SAVAGE GAME

SAVAGE BILLIONAIRES, BOOK 1

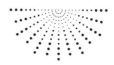

KAREN NAPPA

It is supposed to be one month only.

When Charlotte meets Byron Nolan on her husband's poker night, she has no clue her life is going to change—irrevocably.

When Charlotte Randall enters the room, Byron knows two things:

1. She's wasted on her clueless, arrogant husband.

2. Married or not—she's going to be his.

This story contains elements of abuse and dub-con intimacy. If these topics disturb you, this might not be a book for you.

PROLOGUE

Charlotte Randall placed the tray with snacks on the hall table and checked her appearance in the mirror hanging above it. She looked a bit pale, but her makeup was flawless and concealed the fist-sized bruise on her cheek. She'd styled her hair in an elegant updo with not a strand out of place. She ran sweaty palms down from her waist to her hips, smoothing out a crease in the fabric of the red and white polka-dot dress. Although her insides felt as crumbled and decayed as some ancient ruins, her reflection showed the polished trophy wife of a successful executive in every way. In her thirty-two years, she'd learned to put on a façade for the world.

I hate poker night.

Sighing, she opened the door, lifted the tray, and pushed herself inside the dark room. The smell of cigars assaulted her nose, and she took shallow breaths to avoid coughing. Ice tinkled in scotch glasses, and she slowly walked toward the round table in the middle of the opulent room.

Liam's lecture on etiquette fresh in her mind, she first approached the man sitting on Liam's right side. Waiting next to the man's left shoulder, she held out the tray and couldn't help but admire how perfectly his broad shoulders filled the expensive material of his suit jacket.

Without saying a word, he kept his gaze on the cards in his left hand, and—with an impatient flick of his right fingers—he dismissed her offering. Startled, Charlotte lifted her gaze at her husband, who jerked his chin with an impatient glower. Charlotte swallowed. *I hope I'm not going to pay for this after the guests leave.* Liam's nose and cheeks were ruby red already, which didn't bode well for her, either.

She hurried to the next poker player. Mr. Dennehy wasn't bad as guests went. He didn't leer, didn't touch, and possessed a nice smile.

"Dear Ms. Randall, what are you offering?" Dennehy let go of his cards.

"Cold canapes, sir. I have honey-drizzled apple bites with gouda cheese and bacon, mini-BLTs with prawns, Parma ham and Parmesan cheese on ciabatta, and salmon-cucumber wraps with cream cheese." She bent a little forward to lower the tray.

"Looks lovely as always." Mr. Dennehy selected a BLT with his left hand and popped a salmon wrap in his mouth with his other. His head bobbed enthusiastically as he chewed. Her shoulders relaxed a bit at his silent approval.

Reluctantly, Charlotte continued to the next player. She didn't like Michael, her husband's partner and best friend. He and Liam shared many traits, including their mean streaks and nasty tempers when drunk.

When she lowered the plate to offer Michael a selection of food, he snaked his hand under the hem of her dress and curled his hand around her thigh. She froze and closed her eyes for a few seconds.

Don't show him your revulsion, it will only prolong the inevitable and make him crueler.

Her arms trembled as she forced herself to remain immobile while Michael stroked the soft skin above her stocking and toyed with the garter. His fingers didn't wander higher, and her shoulders sagged in relief when he removed his hand and chose a snack.

Her eyes lifted and landed on the face of the stranger at the other side of the table. Charlotte sucked in a breath as if he'd punched her in the stomach. On one side, horrible scars marred his face, but what kept her captivated was his cobalt-blue gaze.

* * *

Byron Nolan leaned back in his chair and watched as the little housewife scuttled from the room. Liam Randall and Michael Connolly were new business associates and, until now, the evening had been enlightening and disheartening.

His gaze slid to the other man at the table. Although Byron didn't know Ben Dennehy very well, the man had an excellent reputation in the business, and he seemed less reckless and entitled than the other two at the table.

The entire evening Dennehy held back on the liquor and so did Byron, but the other two men indulged extravagantly. With the increasing amount of booze in their systems, their bets became more daring and their play sloppier. On their third round, Dennehy acted as the dealer. It put Byron at the disadvantage of being first, but at least he didn't need to worry the dealer might be cheating.

Like doing business, playing cards was a combination of skill, mathematics, timing, and a little bit of luck, and then there was the most important reason he liked the game.

With poker more than any other card game, it was also about observational skills and knowing when to go all in and when to fold. Byron was a winner both in business as well as at the card table. Sadly, he hadn't played poker with these men before he'd gone into business with them.

Oh well, it wasn't like they'd sworn "until death

do us part". And even that famous oath didn't make it for five out of ten marriages.

Byron focused on his cards—Ace-Queen suited, not bad at all. He dropped two blue chips in front of him. "Call."

Randall and Connolly raised, and Dennehy and Byron called.

After collecting the chips, Dennehy placed the flop on the table—Queen, nine, and Jack, none of them spades.

"Bet." A green chip dropped on the table in front of Liam Randall.

"Call."

As the evening's play had continued, Randall and Connolly kept increasing their bets, and this hand was proving to be no different.

"Raise." Fifty dollars landed on the table in front of Connolly. Byron liked the man even less than their host. Connolly was clearly bluffing, and badly.

Mentally Byron went over the possibilities and took a small sip from his tumbler. "Call." He pushed forward his own chips.

His host raised to seventy-five dollars with a self-satisfied expression. Connolly did the same, but he appeared uncertain now. Dennehy called.

Byron lifted the corner of his cards and peeked at them again, feigning indecision.

"It's your turn, Nolan." Liam swirled his scotch and the ice cubes in the amber liquid rattled in the otherwise quiet poker room as he waited for Byron to answer his challenge. "Don't make us wait all night!" His host smirked, his arrogance palpable in the air.

The guy was too smug for his own good, and after a few hours in their company, Byron regretted going into business with his new partners.

Byron eyed the large stacks of chips in front of him and the diminished piles before the other play partners. Time to raise the stakes.

"Raise." Byron threw in four black chips and lifted a challenging brow.

His host called, leaving him with only a handful of blue chips, two green, and one black.

"I'm out." Connolly folded, tossing his cards down on the table. After he abandoned the game, he rose and got his third cigar.

Dennehy called, took the turn from the stack, and revealed the ace of hearts.

Wordlessly, Byron called by dropping his chip.

Randall tossed in a twenty-five-dollar chip. "Bet."

The fool should have checked first, but it was his funeral.

Byron called. Dennehy folded, collected the chips, and placed the river card.

Something in Liam's cheek twitched, and he shoved two blue chips forward. "Call."

Two black chips landed heavily in front of

Byron. Deliberately, he took another sip and stared his host square in the face. "Raise."

Liam's ruddy face was sweating but his beady eyes were greedy. Liam's eyes dropped to his cards, he licked his lips and eyed the chips. "I can't call."

"Hmm." Byron stroked his chin. "We can work something out."

"I... I..."

From the way Liam's face scrunched up, it was obvious his host was trying to think through his booze-fogged mind.

Liam's face cleared. "I have a Rolex. It's worth more than what's on the table here."

"I'm not interested in your watch." Byron pulled back his sleeve and revealed the titanium Seamaster Diver on his wrist. "I prefer Omega."

"Oh." Liam swallowed and his shoulders slumped.

Byron struck like a cobra. "If you lose, I want a month with your wife, to do with her whatever I please."

Who said kicking a man when he was down wasn't fun?

1

DAY ONE

Dressed in a pencil skirt and a light-blue blouse, Charlotte exited the taxi. Shaking in her three-inch stilettos, she accepted the wheeled suitcase from the driver. She tipped back her head and stared up at the high-rising skyscraper with the bluish-tinted windows. Squinting against the sun, she wondered what kind of job she would get. Liam had been vague about the arrangement, but she guessed he'd told her employer she didn't have any work experience.

Who hires an employee for a month anyway?

Charlotte pulled the suitcase behind her and walked toward the imposing entry with her head held high. When dealing with an unknown challenge, it was important to appear confident after all. She was so out of her depth, it wasn't even funny.

But I will survive. I always do.

After fifteen years of marriage to Liam, she'd perfected her mask and could blend in like a chameleon. Not good enough to avoid the occasional abuse, though. Whatever the job requirements were, it could hardly be worse than the demands Liam placed on her. Right?

A doorman pushed open the glass doors and tipped his head. "Ma'am."

"Thank you." She gave him her kindest smile. What a shitty job, standing outside in a stiff and stifling uniform, opening the door for people.

A nasty voice in the back of her head—a voice sounding exactly like her husband—sneered, *"It might be what you'll be doing for the next month."*

Oh well... Sighing, she pulled the suitcase with her and entered the building.

Pausing for a moment, Charlotte scanned the opulent space. Stunning marble floors covered the expanse, and floor-to-ceiling tinted windows let in the light. A bank of elevators was at the back, clusters of seats were scattered about, and potted plants spread out on her right. Charlotte pulled in a breath and marched over to the reception desk. The impressive gleaming marble counter spanned the left side of the entry hall and boasted three computer screens.

A well-groomed woman with streaked blonde hair in a stylish cut, wearing an immaculately tailored dark-blue blazer over a creamy-white silk blouse with a firm's name discreetly embroidered on the chest pocket, greeted Charlotte with a kind smile. "Welcome to Nolan House, how may we help you?"

"Um." Charlotte let go of her suitcase's handle and stepped forward. "My name is Charlotte Randall for Mr. Nolan."

"Ah, yes, Mrs. Randall. Mr. Nolan informed us about your arrival today. If you would be so kind to wait, I'll get someone to escort you to the private elevator. It's the only one with access to the penthouse." She gestured to the plush seats at the opposite side of the hall.

Penthouse? This is an office building, right?

Charlotte nodded. "Thank you." She opened her mouth to ask for clarification, but the phone rang, and the receptionist turned away to answer it.

Charlotte hesitated but didn't want to eavesdrop, so she turned, pulling her suitcase with her, and dillydallied toward the inviting seats and sofas. Her progress was so slow, she hadn't yet taken a seat when a man in the masculine version of the suit the receptionist wore, with the addition of an earpiece like some kind of secret agent, stepped up to her.

"Mrs. Randall?" He folded his hands in front of him.

"Y-yes."

He moved closer with brisk efficiency. "Follow

me, please." Without asking, he took possession of her suitcase and walked past the bank of elevators toward an obscured door in the corner. After swiping a keycard, the door opened automatically, and Charlotte followed him through and down a long hallway past several doors until they reached another elevator.

Earpiece as she called him in her head, punched a set of numbers in the keypad so fast she wouldn't have been able to recognize the code.

Not that I expect to need it anyway.

When the car arrived, he gestured for her to enter but instead of following her as she expected, he stayed back. "What–" the elevator doors closed, cutting off her question, and her stomach dropped as the car practically lunged upward. It took less than twenty seconds before the doors opened, and she tentatively stepped out and into another long, darkened corridor.

What the hell?

At a loss, Charlotte took a hesitant step forward, moving away from the elevator and further into the dimly lit hall. Halting again, she frowned as she realized Earpiece still had her suitcase downstairs. She was about to turn and get back in the elevator when the doors behind her whooshed closed.

Not knowing what to do with herself, she turned and scanned the area.

If this were some creepy castle instead of an office

building, I would now turn and come face to face with a
serial killer or a vampire.

She almost chuckled at herself but the moment
the thought popped into her mind, uneven footsteps approached her from behind.

Heart pounding in her throat, she pivoted on her
heels and sucked in a lungful of air. A tall figure, his
face obscured by the shadows in the hallway,
approached quickly despite the clear limp in his
gait.

"M—mister Nolan?"

A six-foot-plus frame with broad shoulders bore
down on her. Fighting the urge to run, Charlotte
forced her lungs to expel the air she had been holding. Everything about him screamed power and
wealth and hinted at a cruel and singular intent. She
took a tentative step back and tried not to panic.

As if he caught on to her distress, he slowed,
halted at a polite distance, and tilted his head.

She recognized him. How could she not—the
scarred, blue-eyed man from poker night. She swallowed and forced herself to hold her ground. She
clutched her hands in front of her.

Don't show fear.

Oh, but she was afraid. Not of his scars, but of
the power he exuded. It reached out and encased
her like body heat. Charlotte blinked.

Please, don't tell me I'm attracted to this guy.

She stifled a mortifying moan and stared down

at her feet. No matter how much she willed herself to lift her gaze, she couldn't.

A barely audible huff from him told her he'd moved closer even before his perfectly polished dress shoes came into view.

"Mrs. Randall." The tone of his velvety voice oozed disdain. So did the pause before, "Follow me."

He showed her the backside of his shoes before they moved out of her sight, and Charlotte's brain kicked in. She hurried behind him, almost running to keep up with his long, irregular strides.

They reached a mahogany wooden door, and Mr. Nolan held it open and summoned her to enter. Inhaling deeply and squaring her shoulders, Charlotte slipped past him and fought the urge to pick up her pace. Despite his marred face, he was... attractive, or maybe because of it. His clothing was expensive and didn't hide his powerful body, his scent was seductive and masculine, and he radiated heat and authority. When seated at her husband's poker table, she hadn't realized how tall and imposing he was—

"Please have a seat."

—nor how sensually his voice would stroke her nerve endings. She jerked and then glared when she noticed the smirk on his face.

He had pushed the door closed and leaned his shoulder against the wood. With his arms crossed in front of his chest, an expensive watch peeked from under the fabric of his sleeve—Total arm porn.

Oh, damn, Charlotte, get your mind out of the gutter.

She pulled her stare from his forearms and raised her gaze to meet deep-set cobalt-blue eyes, and the intensity there threw her off balance. Or even more off balance. Her body responded in an embarrassing way. Every inch of her skin came alive as if static energy crackled across it, her breasts grew heavy, and her nipples hardened—all from the sheer impact of his gaze.

Charlotte pulled on the lapels of her blazer as if the thin fabric could hide her reaction or shield her from sexual magnetism and alpha strength.

As she took in his unapologetic stare and air of self-possession, she forced herself to take a seat on the white leather sofa. He was intimidating, and sitting while he stood seemed wrong... no, dangerous. Refusing to give him any more power over her, Charlotte called on her inner core which always helped her in dealing with Liam and waited him out.

He didn't speak or move for a long time, only staring at her and sizing her up.

Does he find me lacking like Liam does?

The thought was strangely disconcerting.

Finally, he unfolded his arms and pushed away from the door. Mr. Nolan stalked toward the sofa.

Despite his noticeable limp, he moved with an animalistic grace.

Her breathing slowed, as if she were a deer threatened by a predator. A predator who was currently looming over her. A predator with muscles rippling beneath his tailored suit. She was no match for him.

Hell, I'm no match for Liam and he's about half this man's size.

He sat down in the chair on the left side of the sofa. The arrangement angled his body in a way that obscured his scarred side from her. Was the man self-conscious about it? Immediately, she discarded her silly thought. He was arrogance personified.

He unbuttoned his suit jacket and leaned back with his elbows on the armrests and his fingers steepled in front of his chin. Up close he was even more imposing, and his relaxed pose amplified rather than dulled the impression of controlled strength and power.

Her eyes skittered around the room and strayed to the mahogany door.

"You're not going to renege on the deal I made with your husband, are you?"

His challenge broke through the fog in her mind and every thought about running fluttered away. Her hands shook, and she folded them in her lap.

I so don't want to know what Liam got me into this time.

She didn't want to go down that path. But she wasn't a coward nor a dishonorable person. Whatever deal Liam had made, she was going to hold up her end of the bargain.

She dipped her head and her bottom lip trembled. "I'm not sure what the deal is."

"Come on, Mrs. Randall, you can't possibly be that dense."

Indignation raised her chin a bit higher. "Liam didn't disclose what I'm going to have to do for you. My husband simply issued the order to be here today and told me I would be working for you for a month."

"Working for me?" Mister Nolan stroked his chin and cocked his head, giving her the full view of his face. "The cowardly bastard didn't explain our deal at all?" He narrowed his eyes. The scars around his left eye pulled in a painful looking way. "For the entire month you're mine to do with whatever I please."

She couldn't have been more shocked if he'd dropped a bomb. Horrible images of whips, chains, and dungeons flashed before her eyes, and her breathing halted before it turned ragged. This man could do so much more harm and damage than Liam, and there were days she could barely walk while under her husband's roof.

How am I supposed to survive a month with this monster?

Because now she knew he was a monster, too.

What kind of man would buy a woman?

What kind of man sells his wife?

They were silent for a long moment, then his amused voice broke the quiet, "And now she is afraid."

Well now.

Inwardly he grinned. His first impression had been she would bolt from the room. His second guess was she would fold and cry.

He angled his face away from her again—somehow unwilling to frighten the pretty little prey who wandered so willingly into his lair. She surprised him, and women rarely did.

Women in his world came in two categories: heartless and ruthless gold diggers who wanted him for his wealth or simpering little submissives starving for some attention and willing to look past his scars to experience his brand of dominance. Neither category could hold his interest for very long, but this appealing little thing didn't seem to fit either category, and the paradox had him intrigued.

When she'd turned around in the hallway, her eyes—green and somewhat tilted like those of a cat —had been cautious and startled but not repulsed or frightened. Usually, if his sheer size and power didn't frighten the little ladies, his marks did evoke at least one of the emotions.

However, when Byron moved to stand in front of her, she'd shown signs of submission but not revulsion. The revelation had thrown him off-kilter, and he'd been brisker with her than his usual self. He was honest enough to confess his usual wasn't hearts and flowers either.

Every time he expected her to falter and wilt, she would raise her stubborn chin and face his challenges head-on. He wanted to bite the pointed chin, clamp his teeth around the flesh and keep her in place like that. Stare her in the eyes and wait for the surrender in them. A surrender that would come. She would submit to him; there wasn't a speck of doubt in his mind. He shifted his hips to give his cock more room as he lengthened and hardened, but this wasn't the time or moment to indulge himself.

The object of his current obsession sat motionless on the sofa, but her eyes had narrowed. Ah. He suppressed his smirk.

There's that backbone and fire I've seen glimpses of before.

Her spunk pleased him.

Byron was tired of women who acted to please him. He wanted real, raw emotions—even when they were ugly. He had the feeling this woman on his sofa buried a well of genuine emotions under the veneer of an obedient housewife and was pleased her bastard of a husband hadn't beaten it out of her. Yet.

Byron didn't allow himself to dwell on the thought. He was looking forward to a month of play. A disconcerting thought crept up on him like a rumor could plummet or skyrocket the stock market on Wall Street.

What if thirty days isn't enough?

Not liking the conflicted emotions and thoughts, he squinted. Time to get this settled.

He bent his knee and placed his ankle on the opposite leg, getting in a more casual pose and relieving a little of the pressure on his dick. He stroked his hand over his mouth, hiding his smirk, as her gaze strayed over the muscles of his thigh bunching and straining the fabric of his expensive slacks.

He locked his gaze on her. She didn't squirm or avert her gaze. A smart prey didn't take their eyes of its predator.

It wouldn't save her, of course, but it made his respect for her dial up a notch. So did his desire to claim, control, and captivate. He wanted to dig under her skin, invade her mind, and bare her soul. He needed to find every weakness and flaw.

"To do what you please?"

Her face impassive, she studied him. Last week-end, when that asshole Connolly slid his hand under her skirt, he'd noticed how she schooled her features, but her eyes couldn't hide her true feelings. Today, tension simmered in those deep green orbs. Shifting again, he took a closer inspection. She might school her features, but the little facial muscles she couldn't control, and the lines beside her mouth and eyes were strained.

She cleared her throat. "I guess I'm not going to clean toilets or do any filing this month, am I?"

Byron thought he knew women, knew what drove them, but Charlotte wasn't like any female he'd met before.

She was submissive, obeyed her husband. If poker night hadn't proven her obedience, her presence right now in his house confirmed it. She seemed to pack more guts and honor in her pinky finger than the fool she'd married had in his entire burly body.

However, she didn't falter under his command. Not many people didn't. It spoke of strength, an inner core he wanted to reach. She was attracted to him. He'd detected how she involuntarily arched her back, thrusting out her chest and exposing her neck. He didn't miss how she ran a hand down a thigh in a sensual caress or how her lips parted, and her tongue darted out several times to touch her lips, leaving them moist and slightly swollen. The lust built inside him. But she was holding back from him, and withholding any part of her body, mind, or soul wasn't acceptable to him.

"Oh, there will be cleaning and cooking and quite possibly some office work as well on the agenda." He clenched his hands, aching with the need to touch and explore and fought against his response to her. "You're mine, Kittycat, and I don't want anybody else in the penthouse for the entire month." He cupped his chin and leaned on his palm. "Having you work as my private secretary has merits, too. Now strip and show me my prize."

* * *

Her mouth dropped open and she froze.

"Need help?" The eyebrow on the unmarred side of his face slid to his hairline.

"No!" She shot to her feet and eyed him as if he were a tiger ready to pounce.

Then he sighed. "I'm not planning to rape you, Kittycat. I want to inspect you. Also… I want to burn these clothes he bought for you."

Burn them? But...

"Earpiece has my suitcase."

"Earpiece?" He gave a low, sexy rumble of laughter and shook his head. "Earpiece! Earl is going to love the nickname you gave him."

"It's not like he introduced himself."

Mr. Nolan stroked his chin, again drawing her

attention to his muscular forearm. His strength terrified and excited her, and wasn't that just dumb?

"Your shoe size outmatches your IQ." Liam's nasty voice reverberated in her mind.

Mr. Nolan made an admonishing sound in the back of his throat and warned, "In about fifteen seconds you get my help whether you want it or not, so quit stalling."

His intimidating gaze ran over her face, shoulders, and clenched hands. Up again.

"Five. Four."

"All right, all right." She held up a hand and kicked off her heels.

He tilted his head in a silent command to continue.

She shrugged out of her blazer, folded the sleeves over it, and placed it on the sofa. She hesitated.

What should I do? Start with unbuttoning my blouse or lowering my skirt.

Again, he made the throaty sound she'd quickly come to recognize as a warning. She fumbled with the zipper and the skirt fell to the floor.

As she bent to pick up the discarded garment, he reached out and stroked a finger over the skin visible through the opening of her blouse. Charlotte sucked in a breath and stilled.

Now he will grope me, squeeze my breasts, torment my nipples. Will it hurt? Will he rape me?

"Soft." He almost sighed the word. "Continue." He sat back in his chair, leaving her wobbling on her legs.

She placed the skirt on top of her blazer.

Surely, he isn't going to burn the set, right?

Uncertainly, she peeked over her shoulder at him.

Eyes half-lidded, cheeks flushed, and his hands loosely curled around the armrests, he was clearly enjoying the sight, and her own cheeks burned.

Damn you, Liam, for getting me into this predicament.

With trembling fingers, she worked the buttons of her blouse, her insides wanting to be done with the little knobs and on the other hand wishing she had a thousand of them. She didn't like how clumsily she was opening her blouse, but if she could, she would have prolonged the moment she'd be exposing more skin to his scrutiny.

She started to turn away to put the garment with the rest of her clothes on the couch as he ordered, "Drop it."

"What?"

"Drop. The. Blouse."

Trembling, she did as he commanded, revealing her torso and the light-blue bra with see-through lace at the tops of her breasts. The undergarment was one of the push-up varieties and made the most of her B-sized breasts. She'd bought it online on a whim in the hope to please Liam. Of course, she never could please her husband.

"Did you wear that for him?" He leaned forward and braced his elbows on his knees.

There was an accusation in his tone she didn't understand. "N-no."

Disbelief etched his features and distorted the scars even worse. "No?"

She shook her head and dropped her gaze. Her voice just above a whisper, she confessed, "I bought it about a month ago hoping it would please him to see me in it, and somehow I chickened out each time I wanted to wear it."

"And you're wearing it now, because…" His voice trailed off, a clear message he expected her to fill in the blank.

"Because I was uncertain about today, and I wanted to feel good about myself." She bit her lip in self-recrimination and wondered why she blurted the truth out.

It always gives Liam power over me.

Giving power to this ruthless man would be worse, and she couldn't afford to give more than she already had to this man. He would devastate and annihilate her without blinking an eye!

Only the creaking of the chair warned her he'd moved, then he lifted her chin with one finger and forced her to make eye contact. "You should feel good about yourself."

Um?

"Nice, your panties match."

The warmth in her cheeks spread to her ears and the back of her neck. "They do." Although he made it a statement, she replied. She fought the urge to drop her eyelids.

Stupid, stupid woman.

He let go of her face and settled back on his seat. "You may keep the set."

Surprised, her head whipped up.

Is he into mind-fucking like Liam?

For a moment, neither of them moved or spoke. There was no deceit in his face, and she inclined her head. "Thank you."

His features softened, and she almost relaxed.

2

DAY TWO

Charlotte wasn't sure how she'd gotten through yesterday unscathed. Mr. Nolan had taken her clothes, and she had no clue if he'd burned them as he'd threatened. The rest of the afternoon had gone by in a bit of a blur. Mr. Nolan had given her a tour of the penthouse, which, in fact, was his living quarters as well as his private office space.

When the tour was done, he'd ordered her to shower, wash her hair and shave—which she'd done without protesting. She had marveled at the variety of toiletries and the expensive cleansing products all from high-end brands.

After she returned to the bedroom, she'd dressed in the French maid's costume he'd left for her on the bed. From running her fingers over the shiny material, she'd been certain the dress was made of pure silk and probably cost more than the ensemble she'd arrived in. The skirt was also much shorter than the one she'd worn, and she'd fought the urge to tug the hem down for most of the day.

However, things could have been worse. He hadn't touched her in any sexual way after running his finger over the swell of her breasts during their first encounter. He did go over his expectations, which mostly consisted of keeping his house clean and his belly filled. She could totally meet those expectations. Although Liam always criticized and berated her, she was a damn fine housewife.

He also expected an hour of physical exercising from her, which had come as a surprise, but was still doable and was nothing to freak out over. At least, there was no reason it would cause a melt-down from her as it was a nonsexual, PG-rated command.

The rest of the requirements were in an entirely different league, and she was so far in over her head it wasn't funny.

Not only did he give her a limits list containing activities which either made her cringe in horror, gasp in outrage, tingle in all the right—wrong—places, or blink in confusion, he'd also given her a journal, and an instruction sheet on poses. Some of those poses had her blushing even now as she remembered them.

Being the coward she was, she'd placed the three items on the little desk in her room, yes, her room, and ignored them for the better part of the evening. All things considered, her situation could have been, and actually often had been, worse, and she dreaded the moment the other shoe would drop.

And now she was procrastinating over breakfast preparations. Mr. Nolan—and wasn't it awkward to live together in close proximity with a man who bought her and call him by his last name—told her he wanted to eat at eight o'clock sharp, but she was hesitant to enter the dining room with his meal. After mental pep talk number eleven that morning, she picked up the tray from the counter and pushed her way inside the dining room.

She froze as he lifted his gaze from the tablet he was reading on, arched the eyebrow on the good side of his face, and tilted the iPad to look at his watch. She swallowed hard, straightened her spine, and marched inside with a bravado she didn't possess.

Fake it until you make it, right?

He gave her a barely noticeable nod of his head in greeting without a word. Only the sound of the antique clock broke the morning quiet as it announced the arrival of eight o'clock.

Mr. Nolan shut down the tablet and placed the device on his left side. Charlotte hurried forward to set his breakfast and a fresh cappuccino in front of him.

"Kittycat," he drawled, "perhaps I wasn't clear in

my explanation, but I want to eat my breakfast at eight sharp, not have it served when the clock has already begun to chime."

"Oh, okay."

His face clouded and she almost took a step back but refrained.

"We'll discuss the correct way of addressing me later today. Right now, I'm late and we need to eat." He held out a hand in invitation.

We? She blinked. "I-I didn't bring f-food for m-myself," she stuttered, afraid she'd messed up more. Her throat ached and her eyes started to burn.

He let out the now familiar hum of disapproval. "Come now, you've done so well until now. You're not going to start with the waterworks, right?"

He didn't sound mean as he said it, more like he was teasing. She peeked up at him. His eyes softened again. He gave her a firm nod.

"Better." He held up a finger, took a bite of the scrambled eggs, and hummed.

A good kind of hum. Her shoulders relaxed.

"Well seasoned and excellently cooked. Very nice."

She inclined her head, not trusting her voice since her throat still felt raw with emotion.

"You may kneel beside me and take food from my hand."

What?

Involuntarily, she took a step back and a half-turn toward the kitchen. "I-I can fetch a plate really quick from the kitchen, Mr. Nolan. I didn't realize you wanted to eat with me." She fidgeted with her apron.

He rested his forearm on the table and ducked his chin until their eyes met. "You did exactly what I told you to do. I prefer to feed you myself. Now come here."

His voice hardened and she stood beside him before her brain gave her legs a conscious order to move.

"I'm a tolerant master, but the food is getting cold and I'm running behind on my schedule." He nodded once at the pillow beside his chair. "Kneel."

Swallowing hard, she kept her eyes lowered and did her best to go down on her knees gracefully. The pillow was comfortable, and she tried to kneel in one of the kneeling positions she remembered from the pamphlet.

"Very good. Right now, I want you in the resting position, do you remember the pose?"

Resting his hands on the armrests of his chair, Byron watched his little kitten settle into a more comfortable position. He wasn't about to punish her for her tardiness. Her entire body screamed tension and fear, and he wanted her soft, pliable, and obeying of her own accord.

Oh, he would punish her, she had too much fire and rebellion in her not to challenge him at some point this month, but right now she needed consistency, comfort, and safety from him.

He took a sip of his coffee and enjoyed the mix of soft frothy milk and the dark, slightly bitter espresso. If nothing else, he would enjoy her efforts in the kitchen, but he wanted more, wanted all from her. At the moment, however, her fear and suspicion overrode her will to submit to him with her body, mind and soul. Nevertheless, her obedience pleased him.

Although she was too skinny for his taste, she looked mighty fine in the costume he bought for her, and it satisfied him more than he expected to see her in his clothes and not something paid for by the bastard.

Charlotte hadn't moved from the Relax pose, but she was anything but relaxed. Having a submissive alert on her Master was a good thing, but Charlotte wasn't concentrating on him. Even with her face cast down, he could almost see the gears in her mind turning with all kinds of scenarios. None of those would come close to the truth, and all of them would be featuring him as a villain, ergo none of those pictures running through her mind were acceptable to him.

Picking up his knife, he buttered a small piece of toast and tried to figure out the best approach. She tempted him to lay her out on the table and feast on her pussy until she screamed, but he refrained. Although orgasms were a sure-fire way to break down a woman's walls and shut down her head, right now was too early for anything overtly sexual.

Instead, he held the buttered toast to her mouth and clamped his lips together against a smile when her startled glance shot up to his face. It took a few heartbeats before she accepted the morsel. His, "Good girl," caused a cute frown to appear between her brows.

Does she realize how much I enjoy hand-feeding a submissive?

He raked his gaze over her tense arms and shoulders.

I guess not.

Forking some egg, he took a bite for himself and swallowed it down with another sip of coffee. He fed her more toast, then frowned at his hand, and kept it in front of her face. "There's some butter on my fingers. Clean them."

"Um." Her eyes flittered to the napkin on the table.

He didn't pull his hand away. "Use your tongue."

Again, her eyes met his. This time her expression was almost pleading, and again, he had to fight a grin. Instead, he tried to give her a blank and unwavering stare.

The lines beside her eyes became more pronounced, but she leaned forward dutifully and engulfed his fingers with her mouth. Awareness shot straight to his dick, and he was thankful the table concealed his carnal reaction to her.

Too soon for his liking, she released him from the warm wetness of her mouth and tried to lower her gaze.

"No. I want your eyes on me during meals."

She jerked like she'd placed her finger in a socket, but obediently tipped her head back.

"Better." He allowed a smile to curve his lips for the first time and almost immediately her expression lost some of its anxiety. She was fucking appealing, and again, he wondered if one month would be enough for him. In winning her from her husband he'd endeavored to take the uncaring, arrogant prick down a notch, but instead, he got himself a little kitten who brought out every caveman instinct he possessed.

Definitely a total mindfuck, but not one he lamented. Keeping her beside him, he finished their breakfast, making sure to maintain eye contact and keeping his touches frequent, but non-threatening.

"Thank you, Kittycat, that was a lovely meal." Her shoulders lowered and he could almost hear the sigh of relief she tried to hold back. Instead, her breathing stayed even and steady, the swells of her breasts moving in a calm rhythm. He admired her control, but he was alpha male enough to view her self-possession as a challenge as well.

What will it take to have her screaming and writhing under me?

Byron forced his attention back to the tasks at hand. He had several businesses to run and contracts and propositions to review.

For years Byron had been driven by gaining power, control, and money. After so many years of chasing the American Dream, he'd achieved everything he wanted, and everything became predictable and boring. He enjoyed the challenge and still derived a thrill from business deals, but nothing sparked his interest for long. And for women... he felt... numb.

At least, he had been until this little kitten walked into their poker game. It wasn't that she was model gorgeous, although she was quite lovely. Something in her demeanor appealed to him on a baser level, and he knew he needed to have her. Right now she was his, and he had a month to own every single part of her.

Byron realized he'd been quiet for a long time as she shifted restlessly, and he cleared his throat. "Clean up breakfast and meet me in my office. I'm sure I can find something useful for you to do."

"I-I could do some cleaning," she offered with a soft voice and downcast eyes.

He looked right through her ploy to distance herself from him. "You could, but I want you near me. How long will your clean-up take?"

"Um. Twenty minutes?"

"Make it fifteen." He turned his wrist and glanced at his watch. "You have until nine-twenty to get your ass in my office and kneel beside me. Not a second later, or you'll forfeit your rights on clothes."

"What?"

Clear indignation rang through the one word, and he grinned. "You heard me. If you don't obey my orders, you lose your clothes."

She swallowed and rose to her feet. "I'll be on time, Sir."

Fuck me.

The "Sir" from her lips stirred the beast inside as well as his libido. The sight of her slender legs peeking from under her short skirt shot right to his groin. His cock blossomed into a thick, throbbing turgid rod. Imagining himself pushing her skirt up and bending her over the breakfast table didn't help the matter either, and he took a few long inhalations to calm down.

3

DAY THREE

Just like yesterday, Charlotte followed Mr. Nolan into his study after cleaning up breakfast. Again, he'd left her alone at night, and his actions during the day didn't make any sense to her. His threat to strip her of her clothes didn't leave her mind, and she'd followed his orders like an obedient little puppy for the entire day. Wiping her wet hands on her skirt, she knocked on the door and waited by his private office.

"Come." His dark masculine voice made her body stand to attention in a way she couldn't control and didn't like.

I'm not attracted to this man.

From the moment she'd arrived at his building, the myriad of emotions left her confused and stole her ability to form coherent thoughts. She had fallen from nervousness of having to do a job she was incapable of doing, to flustered when the elevator brought her to the penthouse, to anxiety and anger when she realized how Liam had sold her to this stranger without any limits to what he could do to her, leaving her at wariness when Mr. Nolan didn't take advantage of the situation.

Oh, the man was domineering, and his sexual intent was clear, but he hadn't done anything inappropriate.

Yet?

Straightening her shoulders, she opened the heavy mahogany door and stepped inside. Mr. Nolan was standing behind his desk, a phone pressed against his ear. As she entered the room, he nodded to her and concentrated on the person on the other end of the line. It left her in the awkward position of having to wait, but she used the short respite to compose herself and study the man in front of her.

"I don't care what needs to be done, just deal with it." He was silent as he listened to something the person on the other end said. "That's unacceptable." He tilted his head back and looked upward as if praying for patience.

Not comfortable with eavesdropping on his phone call, Charlotte tuned out his conversation and fidgeted with the hem of her skirt. This time the clothes he'd laid out for her on the bed were for a red cheerleader costume which consisted of a surprisingly well-fitting sports bra with five thin straps at the back and a tiny skirt that was about as effective covering her ass as a belt. The Calvin Klein thong, of course, didn't cover her butt at all, but the material was oddly comfortable, and even a tiny thong beat going naked anytime, so she wouldn't complain.

After disconnecting the call, he sat back in his chair and settled in a confident, masculine pose. The way she noticed him as a man left her confused. After raking his eyes over her, his smile held a challenge as he patted his right thigh in an obvious come here gesture.

Her eyes widened, and she shook her head.

Uh-unh. I'm not going to sit on his lap. Nope. No way.

Her cheeks heated, and the realization her face was turning beet red only stoked the fire.

His eyebrow slipped up, and her resolve crumbled like overcooked muffins. She stared at his face, fighting the urge to do his bidding. Somehow, his scars bothered her less each time she looked at him. The imperfection made him appear seasoned and strong rather than less handsome.

He tilted his head. "You'd prefer to spend the entire day naked rather than sit on my lap for a while?"

Um, well, when he put it that way.

She bit her lip and peeked at him through her

eyelashes. She couldn't read his face, but the set of his jaw screamed determination. The tight band around her chest loosened and she took a step toward him.

The corners of his mouth lifted a minuscule amount, and she might have missed the movement if she hadn't been trained to closely study the men around her. Her next step lengthened, and his eyes softened. When she stepped even closer, he held out his hand to take hers and tugged her on his lap.

She barely held back the squeak. For such a big guy he moved fast. Even her skills at dodging Liam's fists—mostly—didn't prepare her for Mr. Nolan's smooth move.

With competent but gentle hands, he made her settle on his lap. The muscles of his thighs flexed under her bottom, heightening her awareness of his strength and virility. The spicy amber scent of his cologne held a hint of sweetness without overpowering his masculinity, and she fought her awareness of him as a man. She kept herself rigid on his lap, making as little contact as possible.

Ignoring her stiff posture, he pulled her against his chest. "I want to hold you like this for a moment."

He sounded so lost, and before she could control the words, her question popped out of her mouth. "What is wrong?"

"Some problems at a project in Seattle."

Encouraged by his prompt reply, she prodded, "What happened?"

"Some people are just idiots." He rested his chin on her head. "I just spoke to the general manager of a small factory I co-own. Their accident rate this last quarter was higher than the entire amount last year."

She turned so she could face him. "That doesn't sound good. Those poor people."

His jaw clenched so hard it must hurt him. She lifted her hand to stroke his cheek and comfort him before she caught herself and clenched her fingers into a fist. To her shock, he took her wrist, pried open her hand, and pressed his firm lips to her palm.

"Thank you for caring, Kittycat." He ran his other hand over her back. "Now let me hold you for a moment so I can drain some tension and carry on with my work with a clear head. Allow your soft little body to make me remember there's beauty in this world."

Oh, well. What harm would it do, right?

She allowed her back muscles to relax and her upper body to mold with the hard planes of his chest. The man had no padding whatsoever.

She let out a sigh, and more tension drained from her. Apparently, he wasn't the only one who needed comfort. In some unnerving way, she felt safe and protected in his arms. The emotion was wrong on so many levels, but she didn't want to delve into her strange feelings at all.

She rubbed her cheek against the soft fabric of his dress shirt, inhaling the fragrance of his cologne.

Does he put some on the column of his throat?

She resisted the urge to explore and instead listened to the slow and steady thudding of his heart beneath her ear. Something shifted between them as he teased the soft skin of her inner thigh with his fingertips. She held her breath as his finger trailed an idle path from her knee upwards, but he didn't reach under her skirt or grope her. When he stroked down, she gradually exhaled.

My kitten is a brave and generous woman.

Byron enjoyed the soft skin beneath the rough pad of his index finger. When he invited her to sit on his lap, he wasn't sure what she would do. Maybe some twisted, depraved part inside him wanted her to disobey so he could have her walking around naked.

But damn, she looks cute as a cheerleader. Maybe I should add some dance routines to her exercises?

Today, she wore her hair in a high ponytail instead of the professional bun she'd paired with the maid's costume and the office attire she arrived in, or the chic chignon from poker night. He appreciated the way she adjusted her hairstyle to fit the occasion and was curious what styles she would use with the other outfits he'd chosen for her.

For a few heartbeats, he amused himself by fantasizing about the costumes and the appropriate hairstyle. Today, her ponytail extended from high on the top of her head all the way to between her shoulder blades, and the dangling strands made him wonder how far her hair would reach if she would let it hang free.

This little kitten kept surprising him. Whether he expected defiance or compliance from her, her willingness to listen to his problem and comfort him came as a total surprise. However, he needed to get some work done, and he had a box with old contracts to sort through. A tedious but not too complicated job he selected for her. When he'd chosen the task, he wanted her to do something useful, which she would be able to complete without too much trouble.

He patted her leg. "Thank you for the hug, Kitty-cat." She stiffened, and he grinned in her hair.

Didn't she realize she was snuggling with me?

"I need to get some work done, and I can use your help."

"Oh?" She pushed against his chest and tipped her head back, her green eyes glinting with curiosity.

Amusement tickled the back of his throat—his

inquisitive little kitten. Pity the cat costume would have to wait, but he wasn't going to let her wear it without the tail.

"Can you sort through the contracts in this cabinet for me?"

Suddenly becoming fascinated with her tennis shoes, she bit her bottom lip.

He growled his displeasure. Immediately, she rewarded him with those mesmerizing green orbs on him. "Better." He tipped his head forward. "What makes you uncomfortable?"

Her mouth dropped open. "I… well. I"—she lifted her chin—"I've never done any office work so I'm probably not good at it." Before he could interject, she rushed on, "But I'm eager to learn. I would love to assist you. I'm a quick learner, Sir."

The pleading expression almost undid him. "You'll do fine," he reassured her. He walked her to the cabinet and explained what she needed to do. She listened attentively and it made a man wonder if she would bring the same focus to the bed. The task wasn't difficult, and soon she understood the routine enough for him to let her work on her own.

Returning to his desk, Byron watched Charlotte work for a few moments. Although her movements lacked the confidence of a trained secretary, the slight smile on her face pleased him. Having a task to accomplish fulfilled her. She'd shown signs of a service sub during poker night, and he was pleased to see more of that side from her.

He settled in his office chair and pulled up his to-do list on the computer. After dealing with his accountants first, he arranged for a security audit at the plant in Seattle. He'd just finished a phone call with his HR department about a campaign to attract more IT professionals when Charlotte closed the top drawer and bent at the waist to extract the files from the second drawer.

Instantly he hardened as he imagined getting up and sliding into her delectable little body from behind. Instead, he turned his attention back to the computer. Not only wasn't she ready for him, but he had a conference call to attend in five minutes.

At twelve-thirty, Byron released his little kitten to fix lunch. After they ate, he'd intended to order her to sit on a floor pillow beside him. Given the pleasure she derived from completing the assigned chore, he decided to delegate more administrative tasks to her instead.

By the time they wrapped up for the day, it surprised him how much work they'd gotten done. Not only was Charlotte as quick a learner as she claimed, but she also settled him in a way he never anticipated. Having her in his space made the hours spent working seem brighter and left him more energetic and focused throughout the day.

* * *

That evening when she came out of the bathroom dressed in a terry cloth robe, followed by a cloud of lavender and floral-scented steam, Mr. Nolan sat on her bed. Years of concealing her reactions helped Charlotte to muffle the scream of surprise in the back of her throat, and only a puff of air and a soft, "Oh," escaped her lips.

"You did an excellent job today, Kittycat."

I did? Wait! Did he come to my room just to tell me that?

"Um, thank you?"

He chuckled—sexy and rumbling. "Is that a question?"

He held out his hand, and before her brain caught up with her action, she accepted the silent invitation.

His hand was warm and huge. Using her arm as a leash he tugged her closer, his stunning blue gaze trapping her.

"Let me show you how to thank me properly." His free hand slid to the back of her head. With him seated on the high bed and her standing before him, they were almost at eye level. He pulled her closer until they were chest to chest.

Although he wasn't forceful, he didn't allow her time to think either. His mouth brushed hers, and the fingers at the back of her head massaged her scalp. His lips were strong and sure just like him, and something unexplainable and irrevocable passed between them as she was trapped in the moment. Effortlessly, he coaxed a response from her, and she reciprocated every move of his mouth and each brush of his tongue.

When he broke the kiss, her mind had gone utterly blank. Deliberately, she uncurled her fists from his shirt and winced as she noticed the wrinkles she made in the fabric.

He didn't speak but canted his head to the side and studied her. They both breathed deeply and a bit unevenly as if they had been exercising. Each deep inhalation brought her his warm amber scent. She stroked the creases she made in the shirt, the material between his chest and her fingers doing nothing to disguise the fact his skin was warm and his body hard.

He anchored her with his hands around her upper arms and slowly rose from the bed.

Maybe her brain was still muddled from the kiss, but she didn't feel fear.

"Or maybe you're just not that smart," sneered the Liam voice in her head.

Mr. Nolan edged her away from the bed and steered her to the vanity.

Uncertain about his intentions, she lowered herself on the stool and stared at her reflection in the mirror. Her gaze fell on the man behind her in the glass.

Carefully, he removed the scrunchy from the loose bun she used to keep her hair from getting wet. The long strands tumbled down over her shoulders like a waterfall. Far gentler than his huge hands should be capable of, he stroked over her head and ran his fingers through the tresses.

Giving in, her eyes drifted closed. His fingers were strong, and she wanted to moan out loud as she worked his fingertips over her scalp.

"I'm going to give you a reward, Kittycat." He shifted behind her, and his warm breath brushed her ear. "Lean back."

She complied and his hands kept moving over her head and shoulders, stroking and massaging. His strong fingers found every snag and kink, and worked relentlessly until she felt warm and fuzzy, and her mind had quieted.

She didn't know how long he used his fingers on her scalp, but by the time he leaned forward to take the brush from the vanity table, she didn't even flinch when his side stroked her shoulder.

Standing behind her, he worked the brush through her hair, making her very aware of his suit-covered body at her back. As he continued with long, slow strokes from her crown and down her spine, she timed her breathing to match the rhythmic caresses of the brush. She had trouble keeping her head straight as his skillful hands moved from section to section.

"Hmm, your hair is as long and lush as I imagined. I like running my hands through the strands. They feel like silk. And I love to smell Bvlgari's Thé Bleu on you."

"I like the hint of lavender and other flowers in it. Sometimes perfumes can be overpowering, but these scented body wash and shampoo are great."

When he hummed and continued brushing her hair, she melted into a puddle of liquefied caramel —warm and malleable—and she wondered how her body stayed upright.

With slow, soothing motions he ran the brush through her hair, guiding the strands through his hands—the sound of the bristles running over her scalp distinct in the quiet of the room. For the first time in what seemed like forever, Charlotte let go of her worries and vigilance and relaxed into the moment.

Far too soon, but what must have been at least fifteen or twenty minutes later, he lay the brush aside, and she let out a sigh.

"Like that, huh?"

"Hmm, I do," she replied dreamily. When she forced her eyes open and met his striking blue ones in the mirror, she added, "Very much, thank you."

He smiled at her, bent, and pressed a kiss on top of her head. "You're welcome." Before she understood what was happening, he strode out of the bedroom in his distinctive uneven, prowling gait.

Charlotte sat at the vanity for a long time after the door snicked closed behind him. After his first kiss, he'd done nothing besides take care of her. Her Master hadn't taken advantage or copped a feel. Unsure if his restraint relieved or disappointed her, Charlotte got ready for bed.

4

DAY FOUR

The following morning, Charlotte woke with her heart in her throat and her hair plastered to her sweaty forehead. She couldn't remember a bad dream, but she was as unsettled as after a nightmare.

With a groan, she pushed herself out of bed and headed into the lavish bathroom.

After dropping her sleep clothes on the marble countertop, she went into the walk-in shower and activated the lush water spray. Once the water was warm, she stood under the square showerhead and let the hot stream rain down on her. She allowed the pounding water to wash away the sweat and the stench of fear and let her mind wander back to last evening.

Crossing her arms over her chest, she closed her eyes, and tipped her head back. The water weighing the mass of her hair down felt similar to how self-doubt burdened her conscience. The spray battered her skin as forcefully as her self-recrimination pummeled her mind.

Yesterday, she'd enjoyed her day as Master's personal assistant. She used the flat of her hands to wipe the water from her face.

Not Master, darn it, Mister Nolan, my um... boss.

Heat crept up her neck, and the reaction had nothing to do with the temperature of the water. She wasn't like this, darn it. When she'd entered the room and spotted him on the bed, she'd half expected him to demand, um… other services from her. Instead, he had taken care of her. And she'd enjoyed his attention and ministrations—enjoyed it!

Knowing too well stewing wouldn't help her to calm down and clear her head, she lathered the shampoo in her hair.

However, while she reveled in the dig of her fingertips into her scalp and the lavender and floral scent of the expensive shampoo, it brought back memories of last night. Her thoughts strayed back to the competent rhythm of his hands, his breath against her ear, the tone of his—

Oh, will you stop it! She scolded herself and rinsed the product from her hair.

She worked conditioner into her locks and squirted a dollop of body wash in her hands inhaling the scent.

I love to smell Bvlgari's Thé Bleu on you.

Charlotte slammed a mental door on the memory and reminded herself she was here for a month to honor some deal Liam made.

The last thing she wanted or needed was to get some complicated messed-up feelings for her Ma–

Boss, he's your boss.

She rubbed herself clean, rinsed, and, with more force than necessary, twisted the taps to shut off the water.

He's a boss, who may or may not want to fuck you. Who technically bought you.

She stepped out of the stall and yanked a towel from the rack.

He's an ass.

Just like Liam.

And every other man.

She finished her morning routine quickly. She had only ninety minutes before she needed to serve breakfast. After she patted herself dry, she wrapped herself in the soft bathrobe. Unsure of what he had in store for her, she went back to her bedroom to put on her costume and start the day.

The leather of his office chair creaked when Byron leaned back. Studying the little kitten, he realized she'd been awfully quiet since yesterday. When he'd left her room, she'd been happy and relaxed–even aroused. But this morning at breakfast, she seemed off-kilter.

Was something wrong? Did my retreat after the reward I gave her upset her?

The thought didn't seem logical, but maybe she wanted more. He sure as hell had craved more. But he'd done the gentlemanly thing and left her alone. Had that been a mistake?

Narrowing his eyes, he inspected her more closely. As a businessman, he'd learned to use his eyes, to observe, and not to jump to conclusions. As a Dom, he'd discovered the practice also translated to the lifestyle. A lot of people didn't tell what they needed or wanted, but their bodies showed a person's desires far more often than they realized.

What does she show that she isn't telling?

Dressed in a combination of a harem's girl outfit and a Cleopatra costume, she'd decided to let her hair flow loosely around her waist. While the first impression was sexy seduction, she could also use the length of the locks as a shield. Right now, her long strands hung like a curtain between them, obscuring her face and most of her upper body from his gaze.

Clue number one—hiding expression and body language.

During their time in his private office yesterday, she'd asked questions and kept a close eye on what he was doing. She wasn't blatant about her service but made his work easier and more pleasant with a matter-of-fact approach he liked. She'd showered him with little gestures, which showed Byron she watched him attentively.

Once, she'd slipped a pen that had fallen on the floor back onto his desk. Later, she'd emptied his overflowing wastepaper basket before he could direct her to do so, and by the end of the day, a file he was looking for landed in his hand before he could ask her to get it for him. She did seem to have a sixth sense when it came to what he needed.

Today, however, she stayed as far away from him as was possible in the room.

She was a far cry from the attentive personal assistant from his previous workday and didn't resemble the sweet submissive he'd groomed and massaged last night. Damn, but he wanted Charlotte relaxed and pliable again. He scrubbed his hands over his face before he ran them through his hair.

Clue number two—she is trying to ignore me but is it because she's displeased with me or uncertain about herself?

"You look lovely today and your hair is beautiful worn down. However, it's hiding you from my view a bit too much for my liking."

She stilled, and her fingers trembled as she placed a file meticulously into the cabinet drawer.

Her gaze slid to him, began to lower, paused on his bicep, and snatched back up as if she caught herself doing something forbidden. Her cheeks had turned a lovely pink. Did arousal, embarrassment or displeasure cause the flush?

After a short pause, she straightened her spine. "Thank you, Sir. Is that all? Should I make lunch now?"

"In a moment." He rose, prowled over to her side of the room, and invaded her personal space. "Why are you putting distance between us?" He used his finger under her chin to keep her gaze connected with his. "Aren't we getting along well?"

"Um." With an audible intake of air, she stepped away from him. "We are doing fine as far as I'm concerned, but you're the one who made the bargain." She tipped her head back, finally giving him her green glittering pools of defiance.

Ah, a smile tickled the sides of his mouth; there was his little kitten.

Turns out she hasn't lost her claws.

"It's getting late, and I should make lunch." When she turned sideways and tried to brush past him, he blocked her physical retreat. He stood close enough to snag her arm and halt her movement. If only the mental retreat was as easy to block.

She froze at the contact, and the vein in her neck pulsed rapidly.

"Hold on, Kittycat," he murmured and brushed

his fingers along the delicate shell of her ear and down the column of her throat to her jumping pulse. "You've tried to ignore me all day, just snapped at me, and now you're trying to control how things go between us. I think you've earned yourself a punishment."

She cringed away as if she expected a blow.

Bloody stupid husband of hers!

"Hand me the dress." He let go of her arm and held out his hand.

"No." With a horrified expression, she took a step back, and another one—which made her collide with the filing cabinet.

Byron didn't move.

Biting her trembling lip, she peeked up at him through her lashes.

Cute, but she wasn't going to soften or deter him.

Heaving a sigh, she unbuckled the belt, letting the buttonless dress fall open and shrugged out of the fabric. She didn't look at him as she handed over the belt and the silken gown.

Despite blonde locks shielding them, he could see her small bare breasts flushing with color as her breath hitched. A concave waist flared into hips that would be gorgeous with a bit more padding. Slender legs trembled slightly as her fingertips brushed against her sides. Beautiful yet not enough. He slowly dragged his eyes up to capture her gaze before he dropped his to rest on the thong, and he waited.

Her nipples pebbled.

The muscles in her thighs flexed and the hands beside her hips fisted into tight balls.

Patiently, Byron waited.

Charlotte hooked her fingers in the bands of the undergarment and lowered the scrap of fabric over her hips, down her legs, and placed the tiny patch of lace on his hand.

Then she straightened and gave him his first view of her pussy in the four long days she'd been his. Suddenly, he wasn't hungry for lunch anymore, but she held up her side of the bargain and so would he.

Cursing himself for being honorable, he stepped back. "Be sure to put on an apron while cooking. I don't want any accidents happening with your delicate white skin." Without checking her reaction to his words, he strode back to his desk, effectively dismissing her.

* * *

Still without her clothing after lunch, Charlotte knelt on a pillow beside Master's polished dress shoes as he attended an online meeting, where he convinced three other businessmen to invest in a charity project.

The man can sell ice to an Inuit or sand to an Emir and his customers would be happy and sing his praises.

Her Master was well liked and respected by his peers and so different from her husband. She closed her eyes.

Not my Master. He is Mister Nolan and an asshole who made me walk around naked and kneel at his feet.

She tried to muster up more anger and spite, but somehow couldn't.

Not when he was stroking her hair as he conducted his business.

Tired from keeping her back straight, Charlotte heaved a weary sigh and tried not to lean into him. Somehow, he caught on to her tiredness and splayed his big palm at the side of her head. She stiffened for the briefest moment before she let him push her head against his leg. She shifted into the Relax pose he'd taught her and gave him her weight.

"All right, Demakis. Run the proposal by my marketing team before the weekend, and we'll schedule an appointment next week to discuss your ideas further."

He hummed at something the other person said and sifted his fingers through her hair. "Sounds good." His hand cradled her skull and kneaded, muttering, "Uhuh," before he returned to stroking again. "Yes, have a nice evening, too." He disconnected the call and Charlotte bit back a squeak when he curled his hands under her armpits and dragged her from the floor and onto his lap.

Tilting her chin, she decided not to struggle and carefully kept her expression blank.

"Are you ready to talk about what's gotten into you today?"

Her gut tightened and her mouth went bone dry like she'd taken a bite from an unripe banana. Her mind raced as she tried to come up with a logical explanation, one that would appease him and not hurt her. Each thought getting more ridiculous than the one before, she clammed up like an oyster.

She cleared her throat and turned her head away. An unyielding, but careful hand halted the movement and brought her gaze back to his.

"Talk to me, Kittycat. I need to know what's bothering you so I can fix it."

She pushed against his arm and struggled to wrench her face out of his grip. "There's nothing you need to fix. Nothing you can fix."

Whether from the surprise of her struggle or the venom in her tone, he dropped his hand and she pushed from his lap. He lunged, grabbing her when she stumbled backward and almost fell.

"Careful."

Her ribs seemed to collapse in on her core and tension built in her muscles. "I don't want this," she spat, "Any of this!"

"I think I understand."

Ha. That is rich. I don't understand it myself, how can you?

All she knew was how angry and hurt she felt. How strange pent-up restless energy had her revved up and almost bouncing on her feet like a light-weight boxer.

"You have so much pent-up lust, you can't even think straight."

She shook her head, her mind clouded with anger and frustration. "Ridiculous."

"Kittycat, we've been engaged in foreplay from the moment you entered my penthouse."

She clenched her jaw and crossed her arms in front of her chest. "Just come out and say it. This is your ploy to fuck me."

The muscles and veins in his neck strained against the skin.

She recognized that look all too well.

"I am not going to fuck you."

His eyes flashed dark and dangerous, but he kept his tone measured which scared her even more than Liam in a full-out screaming rage.

He adjusted his hold on her arm so he was beside her and began walking her to the door. "However, you are going to come. I'll give you two choices: one, I can use toys or two, I will use my hands and mouth."

What?

She tried to plant her feet, and to her surprise he

halted. Before she could heave a relieved breath, he planted his shoulder in her stomach and hoisted her over his shoulder. She struggled against his hold and his grip tightened.

He bounced her into a more comfortable position and with a hand on her ass, and the other hand between her legs, all her struggles were futile.

He chuckled. "For all your defiance, your pussy is a tad wet, Kittycat. Pull in those claws and let me take care of you."

The deep and sexy rumble of his laugh made her cream more, and she let her body go limp.

5

DAY FIVE

Warm lips pressing against the junction of her neck and shoulder roused Charlotte. For a moment she felt disoriented, and she swallowed against some strange emotional lump in her throat.

"Are you awake?" His hot breath puffed against the back of her shoulder. "For a moment you scared me, Kittycat."

She blinked her eyes open and squinted against the light. Disoriented, not to mention disconcerted to discover the brightness didn't come from the overhead light but from the sun streaming through the window, she said, "Wh"—she cleared the hoarseness from her aching throat before trying again—"what happened?"

"It seems that not only did you pass out from your last orgasm, but it was intense enough to carry you through the entire night." His voice came within a whisker of sounding smug.

She lay still and took stock of her body. She was positioned on her side, the restraints gone. Master —yes, let's face it, even without him ever specifically stating she was required to address him as such, that's exactly who he was to her—spooned her from behind, cocooning her in safety and warmth. He'd tucked one of his arms under her head and the other lay splayed over her hip… her *naked* hip. Memories rushed back, making her face heat.

After he'd carried her to her bedroom, he'd placed her in the middle of the mattress and effortlessly tied her to the bed. Then he used toys and his fingers and mouth to let her come over and over again, until…

"I feel like I've been dragged behind a horse for miles," she mumbled into his bicep, voice strangely hoarse. She scraped her throat again. Her mouth was dry, probably from all the panting and moaning. She might even have screamed.

Oh, my goodness. I did scream. Never before has a man…

She didn't allow herself to finish the thought, knowing it would lead her nowhere.

Trailing the tip of his finger over her side, he whispered in her ear, "I like hearing the passion turning your voice husky. It's sexy. I like hearing you, period. I like every whimper, moan, whine, and scream."

His mouth was so close at her shoulder as he spoke, she could feel his lips curl upwards against her body.

"But I absolutely love it when your mind is so hazy with lust you simultaneously beg me to stop and not to stop."

Can a girl get more mortified, than this?

She frowned as the chest against her back vibrated with male amusement.

The bastard is laughing at me.

"I don't think I like you very much."

"Oh, I think you do like me. Maybe you don't *like* that you like me, but you do."

The statement could have been arrogant, but the matter-of-fact tone of his voice and the composed delivery made it more an observation—a very accurate observation on top of it. She decided to ignore the words.

"Want to know what else I think?"

"I… I'm not sure."

"I think I need to drive home my message one more time before I let you up to begin the day."

"What?" She stiffened in his arms, and he flexed his hand on her hip in a silent warning.

"You need to know, down to your very core, that I'm going to take care of you. Your wants and needs are my priority. Even if you yourself don't know what your desires are. Yet."

Oh, my goodness.

She squeezed her eyes closed as if she could shut out his words. "Please."

"Please do or please don't?"

"I–I…"

"It doesn't matter anyway, Kittycat."

"I don't want this!"

This time the bed shook with his laughter. "Again, you do want this; you just don't want to want it."

Her attempts to struggle out of his hold got her nowhere, and she let her body go slack again. He was too damn strong, and she was too weak-willed and still evidently way too orgasm muddled to put up a real effort anyhow.

His breath stroked her ear. "I'm going to wring one more orgasm out of you before breakfast. I want to begin my day with your taste in my mouth and your smell on my face."

His words were so carnal and filthy, she gasped. "I can't believe you would think something like that, let alone speak those words." She tried to muster up some anger, but his intentions made her feel valued and wanted instead.

With gentle hands, he rolled her onto her back. He was dressed in different clothing from the day before, telling her he'd left her bed to sleep alone.

Before she could decide how she felt about that, he moved to loom over her.

"You're a beautiful and desirable woman, and I'm going to tell and show you over and over what you do to me, until you believe it yourself."

A battle raged in Charlotte's mind as the words Byron uttered fought with memories of Liam telling her over and over again about how little her small breasts and tiny ass incited him. She had seen the blue pills he used when he fucked her, and she vividly remembered the shame when he'd simply handed her over to his business partner for his own abuse. Michael would sneer as he turned her to her belly stating he didn't want to see her ugly face. The rejection almost stung more than the ripping pain when he violated her back hole instead of her pussy.

She'd long believed she was merely passingly attractive enough to be seen on a man's arm at a function but not sexy or hot enough to rouse passionate thoughts like the ones Byron just mentioned. Thoughts she'd long abandoned reappeared. She and Liam hadn't been married but a few months before she'd begun to wonder if there was far more than friendship between Liam and his best friend. Now... while words were easy enough to utter, Byron's tone and the look in his eyes as he spoke those words gave her pause. Had her entire marriage been nothing but a smokescreen? Had Liam married her simply in order to present a so-called "normal" relationship to the world in order to inherit his father's business?

Byron's hands curled around her upper arms, and he opened his mouth to say something but instead shook his head and let her go. "I can see it in your eyes, you're not ready to accept the truth. We will work on that."

She smoothed her hands over his shirt, not wishing to crinkle the crisply ironed garment. "It's very sweet of you, but you don't have to butter me up, you know." She swallowed and inched her legs apart. "I thank you for the care and attention you gave me, but don't you want to take your pleasure from me now?"

His jaw flexed. "No, Kittycat, I'm not going to fuck you today."

"Oh." The one syllable spoke volumes, and he caught every hidden meaning.

He took her wrists and pulled her arms above her head. On the pillow, he anchored both wrists in one hand and stroked the other down her body.

"Kittycat." There was reproach in the way he spoke her nickname, but also warmth and a hint of pity. "First of all, you are a beautiful, desirable, and sexy woman. You are also smart, sweet, and compassionate. All in all, that's a pretty potent package in my book… and before the month is over, you're not only going to believe I mean it, but accept on a gut level truer words were never spoken."

He adjusted his position and pressed himself against her inner thigh. He was hard, hot and huge. Tilting his head, he bore his gaze on hers. "Even if you don't believe my words, my body doesn't lie. It wants you, Kittycat."

"There are chemicals for that."

He snorted. "No Viagra needed when you're near, Kittycat. My dick stands to attention as soon as you enter the room."

Something between a moan and a sob came from her throat, and she wanted to throttle herself for letting it out. She pressed her lips together to prevent more unwelcome noises.

He leaned closer to nibble and lick at the seam of her mouth until she relaxed under his ministrations and allowed him access. Then he kissed and licked a trail down her body, like an explorer on a mission to find each nook, dip and hollow, and every single one of her hot spots. All her doubts, worries, and thoughts of proper behavior flew out the window.

She lay back with her hands above her head and tried not to squirm as he inched toward her pussy. After what felt like hours, he reached the V of her thighs, and she waited with bated breath for the moment he closed his lips over the sensitive flesh. But nothing…

She lifted her head from the pillow and stared down her body. His face was between her thighs, his eyes riveted on her pink bits. For what seemed like an eternity, he didn't move but just looked. His gaze slid up from her pussy, over her belly and breasts, and connected with hers. His focus burned into her, sending heat through her body, making her skin tingle, her breasts ache, and her labia and clit awaken with a warm pulsing desire.

A slow smile spread across his face, turning his features into the depiction of a devastatingly handsome man, only slightly diminished by the scars.

He propped himself up on his left lower arm and ran his right index finger over the crease between her thighs. She jolted at the soft touch and struggled against the urge to lift her hips, to nudge his hand and direct his aim.

His grin grew as he toyed with her, moved his finger around her slick, puffy folds, and circled the lazy path from clit to her asshole and back. He swirled his fingers clockwise, counterclockwise, never halting his movement and never touching her where she ached for his touch.

Oh, oh, ohhh. She turned her head and bit into the fleshy part of her shoulder to hold in her pleas.

The scar beside his eye puckered, and—with his eyes still on her face—he stroked her clit with a featherlight touch. Still sensitive from his earlier attention, the little bud hardened, grew, and throbbed painfully. She whimpered as she lost the ability to fight her responses.

"Master," her voice barely above a whisper, she pleaded, "Master, please…"

He cocked his head and stroked her thighs comfortingly. She tensed. She didn't want him to take his fingers from her pussy. Unwilling to ask for what her body wanted—no, demanded—she tilted her hips in a silent plea.

Either her tiny movement or something in her expression must have conveyed her desire, because he leaned forward, and framed her pussy with his hands. He pulled her labia apart and slid his hot and wicked tongue right over her clit.

She cried out and jerked her hips, knocking him in the chin with her pelvis. Her gut tightened. "Sorry," she whispered and cringed, waiting for him to explode in anger.

Instead, he chuckled against her crotch and continued licking her. Primed by her previous climaxes, there was no slow building up sensation, and she shot straight into an intense "Holy mother of God what's happening to me" muscles-convulsing experience. Sliding a finger deep inside her, he curled it inward and skillfully stroked over her G-spot while his tongue swirled around her clit. Her abdominal muscles contracted in rhythmic pulses.

Curling the tips of his fingers and using his

thumbs to keep her wide open, he played with her clit and teased the hood. A high, tea-kettle-like sound escaped her, and she couldn't muster the energy to be mortified. Her entire body was burning as little jolts of electric pleasure started to shoot through her.

Ruthlessly, he drove two fingers inside her in a fast rhythm, and her upper leg and pelvic-floor muscles trembled and convulsed. She was on fire, and he stoked the inferno to a blazing heat. She hovered on the pinnacle and held her breath. His mouth closed over her clit, and he sucked with long hard pulls. It was enough for Charlotte to go up in flames like a phoenix. With zero control of her body, her muscles contracted, and her torso twitched.

Everything inside her combusted, shooting plea-sure upward. More flames of passion licked at her skin and burned through her. He kept the sucking and pulling rhythm until the feeling was so intense it became painful, then he slowed and smoothed the cadence to soft, his gentle licks sending shuddering aftershocks through her.

Catching her breath, she just lay there, a phoenix reduced to a pile of ashes until sunrise. After her racing heartbeat slowed to a languid pace and her brain started to function, she noticed how he was helping her to return back down to earth with long and gentle caresses. She struggled to sit up, but

Master made his admonishing sound, and she stilled.

Like the mythological bird, she arose anew from her ashes, but, my goodness, was she tired. Charlotte threw her arm over her eyes and groaned.

Her Master shifted his body and pressed a kiss inches below her belly button, sending sparks down her body, and her abdomen quivered. He chuckled, the vibration against her skin setting off more rippling.

"Breakfast in thirty…"

At her groan, he chuckled. "I suppose I can wait a bit seeing as I've enjoyed such a fabulous appetizer."

This time her groan was more a moan of embarrassment tinged with…

Nope! No way am I feeling a bit of conceit!

"Go back to sleep now, Kittycat. I'll expect you in the office by lunchtime." He gave her a final kiss that ensured she'd spend several long minutes trying to decipher how she felt about it, before he climbed off the bed and walked out the door.

Before she knew it, the entire day had passed. Though she had indeed prepared his meals and knelt at his feet, accepting every bite he fed her, if he'd quizzed her on what she'd done all day, she would have failed the test.

"Go on to bed now," he said.

Her eyes flew to the watch on his wrist to see it wasn't yet even eight o'clock. "It's too early—"

He shook his head, cutting off her protest. "Kittycat, don't argue. You've practically been asleep on your feet the entire day."

"And whose fault is that?" she said and then jolted a bit when she realized she'd muttered the words out loud.

Master's lips slowly curled in a satisfied smirk which she tried to ignore even as her supposedly exhausted body began to respond with a quickening in her belly.

"I left a gift for you on the vanity. I want you to take the day off tomorrow. However, do join me for meals." With a single swat to her ass, he sent her off to bed while he turned back toward his office.

When his uneven strides took him from her view, she sighed and followed his instructions. Even though she gave a quick peek at the vanity, she was too tired and confused to bother with his present or his "take the day off" comment. She'd never had an entire day for herself since she'd married Liam and couldn't fathom what she was going to do with herself all day.

6

DAY SIX

Turned out she didn't have to worry about how to spend her day. Not only was his present an eReader stuffed with thousands of books ranging from the classics to some pretty steamy romance and fantasy books, but he'd also arranged a team of beauticians to attend to every inch of her from the top of her head to the tips of her toes.

Torn between being thankful and resentful, she brushed her teeth and stared into the bathroom mirror. Her hair was now shiny and almost golden, her skin held a healthy glow from body packings, scrubbings, and whatever else she couldn't even remember, and her muscles were more relaxed than ever before with all the massaging and pampering.

Her gaze dropped to her now soft and beautifully manicured hands and fingernails. With all the housework, her hands always were rough, and her

nails never looked nice, but now they and her
toenails were glossy with polish.

However... those were the fun treatments. Less
pleasant had been the waxings. Her eyebrows had
been okay, but then they moved to her arms and
legs and—totally mortifying—ending with her sex—
and goodness, the treatment of her pink bits had
hurt!

Still, most of the day had been relaxing and nice.
True to his words, she didn't have to lift a finger the
entire time. Every meal had been catered and a
cleaning crew went through the entire penthouse,
leaving the rooms so squeaky clean she probably
would have it easy for at least a week.

She rinsed her toothbrush and left the bathroom, thankful for the day and yet couldn't dismiss
feeing a strange sense of disappointment. Sliding
into bed, she tossed from one side to another before
a glance at the door revealed the answer to why
she'd felt unsettled. Despite the wonderful indul-
gences he'd provided, she wasn't the type of woman
who needed to feel as if she were some spoiled
princess. While she couldn't deny being the center
of attention had been nice, she'd missed the challenges he'd given her every day and the feeling of
accomplishment she'd experienced that had nothing
to do with cooking, dusting, or vacuuming.

With a happy sigh, she smiled with the knowledge that tomorrow would find her back with By...

with Master helping him with his work. Or kneeling at his feet or sitting on his lap or perhaps lying...

Nope, so not *going there!*

Flipping onto her other side, she chose to believe that the tingling she was feeling was nothing more than residual sensation from all the day's pampering. Hearing a phantom chuckle in her head, she punched her pillow, closed her eyes, and muttered for a certain cocky man to shut up.

7

DAY SEVEN

"What do you want to eat tonight? Delivery service is coming tomorrow, so there isn't a lot to choose from anymore," Charlotte asked as she peered into the giant refrigerator.

They had a quiet day in Master's office, and she enjoyed assisting him way more than taking care of a household.

I could use the tomatoes, garlic, and carrots for a spaghetti sauce. Did they have minced meat in the freezer?

"Do you like Italian food?"

"Kittycat."

His rumbling voice sent tingles through her body, continued down her spine, took a roundabout at her breasts, making her nipples harden, and sprinted straight between her legs. She pressed her thighs together and gazed over her shoulder.

His attention was riveted to her bottom, and she realized too late how the sixties-style baby doll didn't cover her ass. She snapped upright and bumped her head against a shelf. "Oomph."

"Careful, Kittycat." He pressed forward and with his front against her back, pulled open the freezer door, took out a bag of peas, and tossed it on the counter. He led her toward a stool at the breakfast nook and pressed her down.

Confused, she blinked and tipped her head back. "Do you want peas for dinner?"

"No, Kittycat." He chuckled, rummaged through the drawer with the kitchen linen, and folded the peas into a tea towel. "The peas are for you. Put them on the lump on your head."

Blinking back tears, she stared at the folded package. After Nana had died and Poppa's health had taken a nosedive, no one had taken care of her.

"You know," he tossed over his shoulder in a conversational tone as he walked across the floor, "ice works better when you put it on the swelling. Give me half an hour to arrange some things. I'll put a new outfit on your bed."

Tentatively, she pressed the ice against her head. *Ouch!*

"Why another outfit?"

"I'm taking you out for dinner." After his baffling statement, he marched out of the kitchen, his phone against his ear before he passed the threshold.

* * *

Forcing herself not to fidget, Charlotte waited with
Mr. Nolan in the line in front of the upscale restaurant. She wore a simple, but stylish black Givenchy
minidress that left her shoulders bare and had a
daring cut-out above her chest. The gray belted-
cocoon wool coat Mr. Nolan had gallantly helped
her into fit like it was custom-made for her.

She didn't miss the admiring stares, and she
guessed they made a good-looking couple. Mr.
Nolan was in his tailored business suit with a
dashing red tie and a neatly folded pocket square in
the same color.

"Have you eaten here before?" Mr. Nolan kept
her close to him as they advanced a few steps.

"I don't think I have. But it's crazy busy for a
weekday, which I guess means the food is excellent."
She gave him a short smile and suddenly felt shy at
the dark intent in his gaze. Forcing herself to turn
her attention elsewhere, she went on her tiptoes to
look over the line before them. Resigned, she sank
back on her feet, realizing even on her toes she was
too short to see those at the front.

To her frustration, she was unable to concentrate on anything but the intense sexual attraction
between them, and her attention kept straying to
the attractive well-dressed man beside her.

Forcing herself to turn away from him again

after they shuffled forward for the third time, she watched the line behind them. Next to her, Mr. Nolan did the same and froze as if becoming a statue.

A tingling at the base of her spine alerted her something unpleasant was about to happen. A beautiful dark-haired woman with stunning blue eyes in a white leather minidress angled toward them.

"Byron." Her voice dripped with familiarity, and she oozed sex appeal.

His mouth turned down, but he inclined his head. "Good evening, Kimberly." His arm slid around Charlotte's middle, and he curled his hand around her hip. The gesture was both protective and possessive.

Kimberly followed the movement, and anger flashed in her eyes. "I see it didn't take you long to replace me."

Stony-faced, Mr. Nolan replied, "Two or three dates hardly counts as a relationship, so I don't understand why you would say something like that." The flexing of his grip on her hip told Charlotte he wasn't as calm and collected as he appeared.

Kimberly's beautiful face contorted into an unappealing disgruntled and spoiled expression, red splotches forming on her cheeks. Her angry countenance reminded Charlotte so much of Liam before he struck out, she braced for a blow.

Alerted by her stiff posture, her companion

shifted and firmly pulled her even closer against him. "Looks like the line has moved along and it's our turn. Enjoy your evening, Kimberly." Without giving the woman any more attention, he turned them around and guided Charlotte into the restaurant.

Charlotte glanced over her shoulder and shuddered at the daggers Kimberly was shooting from her eyes at both her and the back of Byron's head.

8

DAY EIGHT

A headache formed behind his temples, and a crippling stiffness in between his shoulder blades crept toward his jaw. Cricking his neck, Byron forced himself to lower his shoulders and unclench his teeth.

He studied Charlotte over the rim of his coffee mug. Taking her out to dinner had been a mistake. She hadn't been ready to face the outside world. After their encounter with Kimberly, Charlotte acted withdrawn and preoccupied, so he cut her some slack. But giving her space hadn't worked before and neither did it now. She needed his dominance as much as he craved her submission.

"Come here, Kittycat." He turned sideways on his seat.

She bit her lip and hesitated.

He waited. Byron didn't have a shred of doubt in

his mind whether or not she would obey or not. He knew the power of silent domination.

When she stepped forward after long seconds, her open and vulnerable expression pleased him almost as much as her willingness to accept his hand.

Using her arm as a leash, he pulled her between his spread thighs and curled his fingers around her hips in a light hold. "I want to apologize for last night."

Her head snapped up. "W—what?"

"I should have considered the possibility of running into acquaintances, and how doing so would make you uncomfortable."

Her mouth formed a perfect "O" and he called himself an asshole and a bastard when her parted lips conjured all kinds of X-rated imagines in his mind. This was not the time to add sex in the mix— not if he wanted her trust.

"I'm not saying I won't take you out again, but let's stay in the penthouse and get to know each other a little better before we venture out in the future, okay?"

When she didn't reply, he squeezed her sides in a silent reprimand, and she jumped and squirmed. "Y —yes, Sir."

He circled her hipbones, and she wiggled some more. "Ticklish?" The corners of his mouth tipped up.

Her eyes widened, and she shook her head like a dog shaking off water.

"Oh"—amusement sparked to life inside him and lightened his heart—"I think you are."

Anchoring her with his hands on her hips, he filed the information away. He would put the knowledge to use later. "Let me feed you, so we can begin our workday. I like having you in my office, little kitten."

"You do?" Opening her eyes even further, she didn't resist when he pulled her onto his lap.

He hummed and scooped some fruit salad and yogurt on a spoon. "Very much so. I enjoy you working with me." He fed her the bite, used his thumb to wipe a dollop of yogurt from the corner of her mouth and licked the digit, liking the taste of her and the yogurt. "You did a fine job with the contracts, and when you sit at my feet so I can touch you and stroke your hair, it relaxes me and helps me concentrate."

After she chewed and swallowed another bite, she gave him a real smile. "Thank you. That means a lot to me. You know, um, being useful and valuable."

He dropped the spoon and pulled her against his chest. She let out a happy sigh and snuggled her face in the crook of his neck, rubbing her head against him like the cat he called her.

Byron leaned back in his chair. His chest filled with warmth and contentment. He rested his cheek

on top of her hair and breathed in the delicious
scent of the shampoo he bought for her. Call him a
caveman but he liked to imprint himself on her.

Awareness flickered at the edge of his mind.

*If I feel this profoundly about her in a week, how
must I feel after a month?*

Second-guessing however wasn't in his nature,
nor was self-doubt or holding back when he saw
something he desired. When being honest—and he
prided himself on always being straightforward—he
was a ruthless bastard when he wanted something.
When Byron aspired something, he pursued it until
he acquired what he coveted, and he wanted her
more than his next breath.

9

DAY NINE

When Charlotte spotted her outfit for the day, she giggled. Her Master presented her with a white blouse, a black pencil skirt, and a black tie. Sheer black stockings with garters and black stilettos finished the secretary-look she doubted was seen in many offices these days.

She shimmied into the skimpy white panties. No matter how she tried to adjust the bra, the cups didn't want to cover her nipples. After her third unsuccessful attempt, she almost wanted to skip the pretty useless piece of lingerie completely but settled on having the underside of her breasts supported by the underwires.

She slid into the miniskirt. Although the black fabric was silk and beautiful, the skirt was so short, the hem played an erotic peek-a-boo with the strip of thigh above her stocking and showed off the garter.

God only knows how much of my ass Master is going to see being flashed every single time I move.

A bit shocked that the very thought didn't have her immediately attempting to tug the skirt down, she shook her head and reached for the blouse which wasn't much better. Although long-sleeved and with buttons all the way to her throat, the material was see-through and didn't leave much to the imagination.

A bit uncomfortable, she moved in front of the mirror to work her hair in an elegant French twist and put on some discreet make-up.

The sight of her own reflection stole her breath away. The strain and worry lines were fading from her face and her body wasn't as gaunt, but the largest differences were her sparkling eyes and ready smile.

I'm happy for the first time since Poppa got diagnosed with Alzheimer's disease.

Not even on her wedding day, when she wasn't aware of how her relationship with Liam would evolve, had she been a carefree and happy bride because worry for Poppa overshadowed that day.

She applied a thin layer of mascara, no need for concealing layers of foundation—her skin held a healthy glow nowadays. After she capped the tube and screwed the lid tight, she almost skipped out of her bedroom, eager to start a new day.

It seems like I'm finally finding my footing.

She grinned and closed the bedroom door.

Even in ridiculously high stilettos.

10

DAY TEN

Until now, today had been an utter disaster. When Master told her at breakfast they would be attending the annual Lewis-Duncan charity event, her hands started to tremble so badly she spilled coffee all over the kitchen counter.

When she packed the dishwasher not forty minutes later, she dropped a plate and the shattered pieces lay in a disarray over the kitchen floor in a resemblance of her skittering thoughts. After cleaning up the mess, she joined Master in his home office and tried to focus on her tasks to no avail. She had to double-check every folder she filed because she was liable to get everything in the wrong place.

"You know what?"

She lifted her gaze from the pile with letter "M" customers and saw Master studying her instead of focusing on his computer screen.

"I think we're done for today."

"Done? But it isn't even lunchtime."

"I know." The corners of his mouth lifted and the scars beside his eye puckered.

She wanted to kiss every line and dip marring his gorgeous features.

"We're skipping this afternoon."

"Skipping? Like taking the day off?"

He hummed.

"You can't!"

"Don't sound so appalled." He chuckled and leaned back in his chair. The leather creaked. "I'm the boss, Kittycat. What makes you think I can't take the afternoon off?"

Well, duh!

"Aside from the fact that you're the boss and in charge of, well, everything? You haven't taken a moment off since I arrived."

"Ah, well now, just because I don't take off very often, doesn't mean that I can't." With a decisive gesture, he shut down his computer and rose. "Go to the living room and light a fire. When you've done that, you may strip and kneel by the hearth."

She gawked at his retreating back and—okay, yes—totally checked out his flexing ass. Was he serious about this? His distinctive footsteps became less audible. He was!

The recognition spurred her into action. She

placed the stack of folders on the top of the filing cabinet and closed the drawer. Then she hurried to the living room to do his bidding.

It took her a few moments before she figured out how to operate the electrical fireplace, but as soon as the flames roared to life, she relaxed. The dancing flames gave the room a cozy and homey feel, despite the vastness of the space.

She stripped out of her clothes and knelt just in time on the white plush carpet when his recognizable footsteps neared.

Taking a deep breath, she mentally checked her posture and straightened her shoulders a little more.

"You're so beautiful like this." He stroked his knuckles over her cheek.

She tipped her head back and her mouth dropped open. Barefooted and bare-chested, he only wore silk pajama bottoms... and carried a bamboo stick at least six-feet-long as well as bundles of rope. She stared at the thick pole and swallowed down a moment of panic.

Of course he isn't going to hit you with that, silly woman! This is Master.

Something must have shown in her face. Master cocked his head and narrowed his eyes and studied her in the quiet observant way he always did. It reassured her even more. He was careful and attentive, not careless and callous like Liam.

"Share your thoughts."

"I'm just glad you pay such close attention to my body language. You seem to realize something is bothering me even before I know it myself."

He hummed and stroked her hair. "Comes with the Dom's territory but paying close attention to my surroundings and the people around me is also ingrained in my personality. I needed it in my youth to survive, and as an adult, I used it to gain power and wealth."

She opened her mouth to ask him about his statement, but he walked to the fireplace and worked the dials. The flames grew.

"I intend to keep you naked here for quite some time, so I want the room to be warm." He shoved the coffee table to the side. "Do you have any injuries or joint pains I don't know about?"

She shook her head. "No, Sir."

"Excellent." Standing several inches over six feet enabled him to reach up and work the rope through a ring on the ceiling before pulling on it.

The bamboo stick rose, and her heart sped up for no apparent reason. "What are you doing?"

"Setting up a suspension rig. I'm planning to do some bondage."

"Bondage?"

His cheek creased. "You'll see. I think you'll like this." He tied the end of the rope around one end of the stick.

She tried to stay in position, but her curiosity made her restless.

Master chuckled. "You really are just like the kitten I call you." He crossed the room to her and squatted before her, his arms casually leaning on his thighs. "How about you take the Relax pose and watch what I'm doing." He rose again and winced, but when she opened her mouth to ask what was wrong, he tapped her nose and went back to the setup.

Charlotte shifted her weight and settled in the more comfortable Relax pose. Master secured more rope to the ring, tied, pulled, and adjusted. Unable to tear her gaze away, she watched the muscles on his back ripple and his biceps bunch.

And here I thought all middle-aged businessmen have a gut like a bowling ball, pasty-white and sagging skin, and a receding hairline.

He grabbed the bamboo stick at both ends and performed a few fast pull-ups. She almost wiped her mouth to check to make sure she wasn't drooling.

When he seemed satisfied, he held out his hand. Engaging her stomach muscles, she rose as gracefully as possible. When she reached him, he pulled her into his arms, and his firm lips connected with her mouth in a hard kiss. She opened for him and stroked her tongue against his. His arms flexed, and she melted against him. In his signature way, he kissed a path over her jaw toward the sensitive spot between her left ear and her shoulder. Weak-kneed, Charlotte sighed and arched her neck to give him more access.

When he pulled back, his eyes were almost black and smoldering. "Do you trust me?"

She curled her arms around his waist and tipped her head to look at him. "With my life, Sir."

He threw back his head and bellowed a laugh. "That might be excessive, Kittycat."

Wrenching her stare from the devastating man in front of her, she moved her gaze over the suspension rig before her attention shifted to the piles of rope on the floor. He reached for a bundle, and with one tug on the knot it uncoiled, falling to the floor, leaving him holding the folded half.

He pressed his chest against her back, and she leaned against him. "You must know that I have EMT shears here, so if something hurts or bothers you, I'll have you down in no time. Okay?"

She reached her arm up, curled her hand behind his neck, and stared up at him. "I love how careful and considerate you are."

He pressed their cheeks together. "I'm serious. I can only adjust something if you tell me. Don't hold out on me. I will be touching you a lot. That's not because I'm a pervert." He sucked her earlobe in his mouth, and she could swear she felt the pull on her clit. "Well, okay, not *just* because I'm a pervert, and I like to run my hands all over your body." He paused to emphasize this wasn't a joking matter to him. "My main objective is to check your skin temperature and make sure I'm not causing you harm."

"Oh, okay."

He ran his hands along her arms, trailing the rope over her skin. The smoothness surprised her. Tightening his hold on her arms, he brought her hands behind her back. With stunning competence, he tied her arms together and looped the end of the line over the bamboo hanging from the ceiling. Sensually running his hands over her shoulders, he circled her and tied the end of the rope around her wrists.

"Tug on the bindings."

She did. Although she had some freedom to move, he'd tied her securely.

"Still all right?"

"Yes." She considered her answer for a moment. "Yes, I am."

He wound another rope around her torso, around her ribs, above and under her breasts, and around her again. The harness lifted and compressed her breasts. The ropes hugged and held her like they were an extension of his arms. She relaxed as more rope circled her body and sensitized her skin.

He stroked her hair and whispered, "You're lovely in my ropes," in her ear. Her head lulled back against his shoulder. In a soothing glide, his hands roamed over her, testing the bindings and assessing her skin.

So competent, so careful... love him...

She drifted on endorphins, her mind more at peace than she'd ever remembered being, but her awareness of her body heightened. With her eyes closed in utter bliss, all her other senses were engaged. The touch of the ropes and the strokes of his hands on her skin were comforting and erotic. He smelled of fresh cologne and virile male. The rushing of the flames in the hearth, the scraping of the rope over her skin, and the rustling of his silken pants as he moved around her, caressed her ears in comforting waves. Her breathing slowed and synchronized with his, without her even trying.

"Look at you, utterly in rope space, aren't you?" He pressed a kiss to the curve of her shoulder, and the tender gesture shot a shiver of pleasure down her spine. "Cold?"

What?

"Hmm? No." Sluggishly she moved her head from side to side. "No, I'm fine." She opened her eyes and turned her head so she could see his face. She smiled at him.

He kissed her temple, and with his hands curled around her biceps created some distance between their bodies. A disappointed sound between a whine and a grunt left her throat.

Master picked up a new piece of rope and chuckled. "Just need some material and a bit of space to work." He knotted it at her back and looped the end over the stick hanging from the ceiling.

Sitting on his heels beside her left leg, Master caressed her calf and lingered on the sensitive spot behind her knee and on the curve below her buttock. She could swear her entire body turned into a furnace and every touch dialed up the fire. Following his hands, he trailed kisses from her knee to her thigh and looped the rope twice around her upper leg, about a hand's width above the knee. The end went over the bamboo as well. He pulled her leg up high in the air and made her balance on her right leg like a ballerina performing an arabesque.

"Are we still okay, Kittycat?"

"Absolutely, Sir." There wasn't a moment of hesitation or an ounce of doubt in her mind. She was safe and cared for by a marvelous man and a wonderful Master. He pulled her leg even higher, but she wasn't scared at all.

After fetching more rope, he secured her other leg in the same fashion he had her left and tossed the end over the stick. He pulled, and with the support of his other hand under her right leg, he lifted her in the air.

Her stomach dipped and she tensed for a

moment before she settled. The ropes would hold her. She let out a contented hum.

He cradled her face in his hands. "Open your eyes."

Huh?

"Open. Your. Eyes."

The command in his voice made her eyes pop open. and she met his stare. "How are you doing?"

"I'm great. Just peachy."

"Peachy, huh?"

His mouth twitched and she wanted to stroke the corner—couldn't move.

He brushed his lips lightly over hers, and moved out of her vision, trailing his hand over her neck, shoulder, down her arm to her hand.

"Squeeze my fingers." He placed two digits in her palm, and she obeyed. "Excellent, kitten, that's great. Any tingling or numbness?"

"No. Not really. The rope feels good. So good." The last word ended on a moan.

"Okay, Kittycat, I'm going to keep you like this for a little longer before I untie you for some cuddle time. Call out if something is starting to hurt or if you're getting uncomfortable before that, okay?"

As Charlotte allowed the ropes to hold her, she didn't mind she was naked and bound. She didn't feel embarrassed or frightened. Not sure how long he kept her suspended, she was floating in a happy place. Even when he lowered her to the rug and

almost reverently removed the ropes, her mind
hummed with contentment. When he stretched out
beside her on the rug and simply cuddled her,
spooning her back to his chest, her soul soared.
With the fire warming her from the front and
Byron's body-heat at her back, her insides were
warm and gooey, and her heart almost burst with
happiness.

11

DAY ELEVEN

More nervously than a teenager going on a prom date, Charlotte exited her bedroom in the stunning ivory-white gown. The off-the-shoulder embroidered bodice made the most of her small chest, and the hairstylist had blow-dried her long locks in soft waves.

A little insecure on the ridiculously high, nude Christian Louboutin evening-wear sandals with the peep-toe fishnet panel and straps, she went in search of... Byron. Tonight, she would be his date, not his plaything slash prize of the month but a date.

Don't call him Master or Sir, you dummy.

Concentrating on staying upright and trying not to panic over tonight's task, she wandered into the living room and stopped dead in her tracks. Standing at the tall window, Ma... Byron was dressed in a single-breasted midnight blue tuxedo. Where Liam always resembled a fat penguin in a dinner jacket and his cummerbund never seemed to fit, this man filled the attire like he was made for it. He half-turned and she frowned, his bowtie was still hanging limply around his neck.

Doesn't he know how to tie it?

"Charlotte." His gaze and his voice were warm as he pulled his hands from his pockets and prowled over to her with outstretched hands.

She closed the distance, let her hands be engulfed in his warm grip, and accepted a kiss on her cheek.

"You are absolutely stunning in that dress, Kitty-cat. How are the shoes?"

"Surprisingly comfortable, although I'm afraid I will trip."

He gave her a dazzling smile. "Just hang on to me. I won't let you fall."

Oh, how I wish I could hang on to him for real.

Because what he said was true. He wouldn't let a woman in his care fall or come to harm. She forced the wishful thoughts aside and distracted herself by stroking the satiny lapels of his dinner jacket. "You look dashing in a tux, Sir." She tapped the tie end with a manicured nail. "Do you need help with that?"

He narrowed his eyes on her and studied her for a long time. Then he inclined his head. "I would like that, yes. Do you know how, or do I need to guide you?"

A smile took over her face as she remembered Poppa. "My grandfather wore a bowtie on a daily basis for my entire childhood. As soon as I mastered lacing my shoes, he taught me how to knot his tie." She finished the knot and rested her hands over it. "Later when his arthritis became so bad, he couldn't handle the most basic things himself, and I did his bow tie every day." Her voice trailed off and she stared out of the window without actually seeing anything of the scenery.

"What happened to him?" Comforting hands stroked over the three-quarter sleeves of her dress, keeping the cold threatening to wash over her at bay.

"What happens to old people? He died." She straightened her spine and pulled on the reins of her emotions. "My mother wasn't married when I was born and... um... couldn't cope with a baby. My grandparents took me in. Nana, my grand-mother, died when I was twelve and from that time on, it was just Poppa and me. He took care of me until he couldn't anymore, and then I took care of him."

He curled his hand around her cheek and forced her to face him. "How old were you?"

"Just before my junior year, Poppa was diag-nosed with Alzheimer's. I cared for him for about a year before I couldn't handle his care, footing the bills, and going to school all at the same time."

He tilted his head like a graceful animal listening. "Why do I have the feeling this isn't all?"

Her shoulders slumped. "You're right. Liam was our landlord's son and was responsible for collecting rent. When we couldn't pay him on time for several months, he suggested a deal. He needed a wife to make his daddy happy, and I needed money to take care of my grandfather."

"And so you married him."

Charlotte stayed silent for long moments, her gaze returning to the past as easily as looking beyond the glass of the windowpanes, before she nodded and whispered more to herself than him, "Yes, so I married him."

* * *

Hans, his private chauffeur, halted the Tesla Model X on the one-way street opposite the main entrance of the Grand Plaza of Union Station. Charlotte seemed mesmerized by the choreographed patterns in the Henry Wollman Bloch Fountain, but Byron suspected she was gathering her resolve. She'd voiced her qualms about being his plus one for the gala, but he overruled her objections.

A uniformed valet rushed forward to open the back door and came to a skidding halt when Hans engaged the falcon-wing back doors. The corners of Byron's mouth twitched. Somehow it seemed like he found enjoyment in a lot of things and discovered his sense of humor these days. Byron slid out of the sleek car before turning to help Charlotte exit from her seat.

He nodded at Hans and the gawking valet before guiding his date to the entrance of the swanky building where the annual gala for the Lewis-Hawkins Foundation would be held. With twelve hundred seats it was one of the bigger autumn events for Kansas City's rich and influential.

Set up by the medical Lewis-Hawkins family, its purpose was to give talented and unprivileged students a medical school scholarship. Although many attendees used the gala to expand their professional network and to see and be seen, for Byron the cause was more personal. Coming from North Kansas City and growing up there, Byron had intimate knowledge of the struggle to better himself.

His gaze slid to the stunning woman beside him. Her revelation about her upbringing explained much about her, even her relationship with the bastard husband. The reminder of Liam Randall brought out the possessive caveman in him, and Byron splayed his fingers on the small of Charlotte's back to make as much contact as possible.

Keeping a close eye on Charlotte, Byron led her

through the crowd and discreetly exchanged some business cards. He might like the charity, but he wasn't a fool to pass up any chance to further himself either. Slowly they were making their way through the crowd toward the tables exhibiting the to-be-auctioned items, when he spotted Doctor Gregory T. Lewis and his wife Doctor Sandra Duncan-Lewis.

"Ah, Nolan," greeted Gregory. "Always a pleasure to have you. I hope you and your companion will have a pleasant evening." His eyes slid to Charlotte and narrowed. "Good evening, Miss…"

"Charlotte," she hurried to say. "Good evening to you, too." She nodded politely at Mrs. Lewis, who smiled but didn't speak.

The stunning brunette wasn't a wallflower by any means, but Byron knew she was submissive to her husband and preferred to hang back at events like this.

Gregory cleared his throat. "I hope you have your checkbook ready, Byron. Please check out the wonderful items we have in the auction, including a one-week skiing vacation in Aspen for two." In a friendly but also a bit forced fashion, he clapped a hand on Byron's shoulder. Before Byron could dig into the matter, other attendees vied for the hosts' attention.

"Thank you, I will." He inclined his head. "Mrs. Lewis." He led Charlotte closer to the table. In the past, he wouldn't be interested in a trip for two. Right now, he wondered if Charlotte liked snow.

* * *

Relieved to be away from the prying eyes of the Lewises, Charlotte let her escort lead her toward the auction tables. Sandra Lewis had totally recognized her and probably so did her husband. How mortifying!

She only half paid attention to the items on display and kept casting furtive glances at the people around them—knowing they would run into more people she was acquainted with. She should have been more adamant about not attending. But how could she when he was so caring for her and clearly wanted her to escort him.

Maybe I'm a masochist and I like people—men—to trample all over me?

"Nolan."

Byron and Charlotte slowly turned and faced Ben Dennehy.

A smile softened Mr. Dennehy's face. "Mrs. Randall, you appear to be doing well." He shot Byron a glance, which seemed to hold a wealth of meaning, but whatever he communicated went past her.

She glanced over to the man beside her and

caught the nod he gave Mr. Dennehy. Apparently, he did understand the other man's expression.

"I'm pleased to see you both." Mr. Dennehy caught Charlotte's hands and kissed her on her cheek. "The two of you seem well suited and happy together."

Charlotte blinked and furrowed her brow. What did he mean by that comment? She slowly exhaled as Byron and Mr. Dennehy engaged in business talk. She might have been interested in the topic but, truthfully, she needed a little space to pull herself together. Although all the guests were courteous, Charlotte hadn't missed the inquisitive glances and the soft whispers.

Will they all consider me a money-grabbing whore?

It was bad enough Liam and Michael viewed her like that, but for friends and acquaintances to think so lowly of her was another blow. She moved a little away from Byron. Ruining her reputation was one thing but dragging him down with her was another. She feigned interest in something at the far end of the table and eased further away. Byron and Mr. Dennehy were still engrossed in their conversation. Excellent.

Suddenly, a painful grip around her upper arm and a hard pull forced her to turn, and she came face-to-face with Liam.

Of course he's here.

She tugged on her arm to no avail. The action

only made him dig his fingers in deeper and she winced.

Smirking, he raked his beady eyes over her body. As he leaned toward her, she recoiled from the reek of liquor oozing from him. Even this early in the evening it was obvious Liam had imbibed heavily, and he swayed a little on his feet.

"My, my, my. Don't you look dashing, flaunting around on the arm of another man?"

Charlotte closed her eyes as she fought back the nausea threatening to overwhelm her. It is just like him to be angry at her for something he'd arranged himself. She swallowed, centered her breathing, and deliberately made eye contact. "Good evening, Liam. I hope you'll have a pleasant night." She began to turn her head to Byron, but the nails of his hand pricked her arm, and she worried he might rip the beautiful dress.

He pulled her closer and glared at her. "Don't try to dismiss me like that, you pathetic little whore. Maybe you think you're something in the fancy clothes and shoes, but you're still the one who fucks for money." He spat the words at her, and spittle hit her face and chest in wet, warm splotches. "You're my bitch of a wife, and in about two weeks you'll pay for your arrogance."

Her esophagus burned with the bile threatening to rise, and the enraged expression on Liam's face scared her, but her fear didn't even come close to the terror threatening to pull her under when he whispered with menace, "I'll make sure Michael will be there to welcome you home, fucking cunt."

Blood roared in her ears as Byron and Mr. Dennehy sidled up to her sides and flanked her.

"Is there a problem here?"

Byron's voice sounded almost as menacing as Liam's had. Only where she wanted to run and hide at Liam's tone, Byron's made her feel safe and wanting to burrow into his embrace.

"Nope." Liam popped the '*p*'. "Not a problem whatsoever. Just a little heart-to-heart with my wife." He sneered at them both, "Enjoy your time," and staggered away, bumping into a couple before the crowd swallowed him.

12

DAY TWELVE

Around two o'clock in the morning, they returned to the penthouse. Byron thanked Hans and bid him good night before pulling a near-catatonic Charlotte from the Tesla. With his hand on the small of her back, Byron guided her through the side entry and into the quiet hall.

Their footsteps echoed through the silent corridor, hers a light and fast click-clack, his footfall heavier and uneven despite his effort not to favor his knee. Charlotte was white and withdrawn and only a ghost of the vibrant woman who had enhanced his home and improved his life for nearly two weeks now.

She stayed subdued as he led her into the private elevator and didn't say a word as they entered his home. Robotically, she allowed him to guide her through the penthouse and into his bedroom—their bedroom!

Damn fucking Liam Randall! He was going to rip the little bastard apart like the fucking asshole did his woman—his being Byron's—not Randall's. She might legally be bound to the cruel sonofabitch right now, but her mind, body, and soul belonged to him.

Byron was done pussyfooting around. Time to take off the gloves.

She's mine.

He held her head between his hands and took hungry possession of her mouth. Taking full advantage of her small gasp, he swept his tongue in. Her small hands fisted on his shoulders, but she didn't push him away. He slanted his head and drew her tongue into his mouth, giving her his in return. Not letting her go, he feasted on her lips and tongue as he'd wanted for almost two weeks now. Being secured and overpowered didn't frighten her, he would bet his extensive stock-market portfolio on it. She enjoyed the hell out of his control.

He let go of her face and roamed his hands over her shoulders, down her arms, where he shackled her wrists and brought them to the small of her back. She arched into his hold, and her breasts brushed against his chest. Distracting her with kisses to her neck and jaw, he used his size and bulk to press her backward toward the bed.

She gasped when the mattress hit the back of her legs, and he claimed her mouth again. She practically melted under the sensual onslaught. He pressed on, letting go of her hands, so she could brace herself on the bed, and he followed her down, still kissing, nibbling, and sucking on her tongue and lips.

When he tried to pull back, he noticed he couldn't. Charlotte had wrapped her arms and legs around him like a vice. Caressing her limbs, he untangled them carefully and propped himself up to one elbow so he could see her face. Her pupils were dilated, and her face and neck were flushed. She showed all the signs of an aroused woman—still...

"I want to make your body tremble with pleasure, and I want you to drench the bedding with your juices. Are you all right with that?"

Her back arched, and her nipples pebbled into hardened points. Indulging them both, Byron stroked the back of his hand over the extended tips, making sure to keep the touch light as a feather, as he waited for her answer. She licked her lips, and more heat ignited in him.

"You're asking?" she whispered. Her darkened eyes widened.

"Yes, Kittycat, I'm asking. As I told you at the beginning, I want all of you, but I'm not going to take what you don't want to give." He dropped a kiss to her nose, the tender gesture pushing away some of the tension in her body.

"All–All right."

"Since I don't think you're ready for fucking, I want to limit tonight to light bondage, mouth and fingers, and toys."

She just stared at him unblinkingly.

"Kittycat."

She blinked.

"Do you have any problems with my plans?"

She slowly shook her head, looking a bit dazed. "N-No?"

He snorted a laugh. "Is that a question or an answer?"

Something in her eyes flashed, and her lips firmed.

Ah, and here we have the hissing and spitting little kitten she is.

"No, I don't have problems with your stuff, ah, list, ah, plans. I'm just, um, I wasn't expecting you to ask me anything. You own me for a month, right?"

"Nonconsensual sex is rape, Kittycat, no matter what you call it."

"Nonconsensual? Liam agreed. He—he told me to be here." She bit her lip and glanced around as if the answer to her question was written on the walls.

"Kittycat." He placed a wealth of empathy in his voice as pain stabbed his chest.

Fucking Liam Randall, impotent, cowardly...

His inner rambling and—quite honestly murderous—thoughts toward her husband came to a halt when he detected her scrambling away from him on the bed. "Shh. I'm not mad at you, sweetie. Shh."

She pursed her lips and her brows lowered, but she stopped putting distance between them. Tension rolled from her in almost tangible waves.

Great job, Nolan. Even when you try to negotiate with the pretty Kittycat, you manage to terrify her.

To his amazement, a small hand slid into his palm and squeezed. He turned his head and faced her.

"I'm not afraid of you. I'm afraid of angry men, and you just looked angry."

"Oh, Kittycat." He curled an arm around her and pulled her against his body. She came willingly and even draped a leg over his thighs. His body responded instantaneously, but if she noticed, Charlotte didn't react. Byron pressed a kiss to her head and chuckled in her hair. "How about we try this again?"

Against his chest, her cheek rose. "All right, Sir. Negotiation?"

Her voice was a bit muffled against his skin, and he couldn't see her face, but maybe it was easier for her if she couldn't see him. "Go ahead."

"I agree to what you suggested, and I would like to add a blowjob, and I'm not averse to sex, but I would like to play that by ear if that's all right with you?"

He flexed his hand laying curled around her shoulder and forced himself to relax his hold when his fingertips made white indentations on her delicate skin. "I agree. However, I want you to have a safeword for when things get to be too much. Use red if you want everything to stop, and yellow if we need to slow down."

"Can't I just say no or slow down?"

"Kittycat, contrary to popular belief, no doesn't always mean no. Sometimes, we say no because we're overwhelmed, and sometimes, we protest because we think we shouldn't like what's happening."

"Oh, okay. Red to stop and yellow to slow down. I understand, Sir."

One moment she lay half draped over him cuddling, the next she was naked as a jay bird, flat on her back with Sir looming over her. He didn't frighten her, not exactly, but the intensity in his expression took her breath away.

His intense blue gaze darkened with desire, and she marveled at her ability to evoke such lust. When Liam fucked her—or let Michael use her—she was nothing but a convenient hole. The way Sir viewed her was different.

"What was that thought?"

She jerked. "W-what?"

"I want to know what put that expression on your face."

She fought back the tears. "L-Liam. How... how differently you treat me from him."

He let out an animalistic growl. "That man is not worth a moment of your thoughts and definitely has no place in our bed."

She blinked at his use of *our bed*, and a wayward tear found its way to the surface and trickled down her cheek. Using the pad of his thumb, he wiped the drop from her skin and cradled her face in his palms.

His mouth landed on hers, and an "Oomph" escaped her as their teeth clashed. His tongue slid inside, seeking hers, almost dueling with hers before they settled into a more languid exploration of each other's mouths and tastes. A warmth, partly satisfaction, and partly arousal, built in her chest, and by the time he pulled back, she was as soft and warm as freshly cooked noodles.

Charlotte bemoaned the loss of his body weight on top of her and wanted more of his taste. She reached out for him and discovered she couldn't.

Sir sat back on his haunches and smiled

wickedly as she struggled against the bindings he'd used to cuff her to the headboard.

Her heart slammed in her chest like a frightened, caged animal's. She was naked, tied to a bed, and at the mercy of a still completely clothed man she barely knew. She froze and couldn't look away from him.

Did I make him mad? Please, don't hurt me.

He tilted his head without a trace of anger in his demeanor. Exuding determination and patience, he had that confident *I'll wait while you panic, but I expect you to conquer your fear* countenance he'd adopted several times now during her stay with him.

Releasing the breath she'd been holding, she forced her muscles to relax. "I'm-I'm okay."

His brow furrowed, and his scars puckered. Charlotte wanted to stroke and kiss that marred skin. The silly idea she could take away his pain fluttered through her mind, but the skin was healed, and the white lines indicated whatever gave him those marks had happened a long time ago. She wanted to ask what happened but didn't dare.

He stroked his hand from her foot to her knee and back and remarked softly, "You know, this was a moment for you to use yellow or red, but I don't think it ever occurred to you."

"Ah."

His cheek creased. "Thought so. Let's add green for a go-ahead, shall we?"

Something dawned on her. "It's like traffic lights."

"Exactly." His teeth flashed white against the day's worth of stubble on his cheeks. "So what color are you now, Kittycat?"

She took stock of her body. Her heart was behaving, and her cuffed hands didn't consume her thoughts any longer. "I'm nervous but not afraid. Green." She lifted her gaze to him. "My color is green."

"Brave little Kittycat."

Sir pressed a sweet kiss to her lips before he moved over her jaw, caressing her skin with butter-soft velvety lips. Seemingly content with exploring her skin, nuzzling, and suckling, he moved at a snail's pace to the sensitive spot where her shoulder met her neck. Charlotte canted her neck to the side to give him more access, marveling at the time he spent on simply kissing and tasting her. This fore-play had already taken more time than Liam's entire idea of lovemaking, and that was before he grew cold, distant, and cruel toward her.

A pinch on her nipple made her gasp and arch her back. She panted as Master didn't let go of the sensitive peak but held the pressure. She squeezed her eyes shut and pressed her lips together against the plea wanting to escape.

"Color?"

Involuntarily, she shook her head.

"Say it."

"Y-Yellow."

Immediately, he eased the pressure. "Didn't I order you to leave him out of this bedroom?"

She wanted to curl up in a shameful ball, but both the cuffs and his body prevented her from moving, and she couldn't even hide behind her long hair, every inch of her body exposed and vulnerable. "I'm sorry. I-I don't want to think about him, but…" she broke off the sentence, not knowing how to continue.

He licked over the nipple he'd just abused, and natural lubrication slickened her inner thighs.

He hummed against her breast, sending shockwaves of sensation through her. "You like it when I put my mouth on you."

It wasn't a question, but she nodded anyway.

"Spread your legs for me."

Too shy to blatantly flash him, she inched her feet apart and tried to keep her knees together.

He tipped his head forward and drew his brows down. It was all the reprimand she needed. She didn't want him there, but then she really, totally did.

She let out an uncontrolled moan and dragged her thighs apart.

"Very pretty."

Pretty? No woman was pretty down there, now, was she?

He ran a finger over the crease between her leg and her pussy. His touch was so light it almost tickled, but his stroking finger also felt amazing. More wetness slickened her opening, and she could feel some trickling between her buttocks.

Circling the one finger around her labia, he… played, and she tried not to squirm. Of course, she didn't stand a chance against his resolve, and before she knew it, her lower half was wiggling on the mattress.

"You know…" His tone was conversational, and his finger never stopped the torturous, sensual assault.

Charlotte couldn't believe it. She was drenching the bedding even without him touching her clit, never once penetrating her.

"I do think you move around too much. Are you ready for more restraints?"

Yes! Oh god, no!

He chuckled and skimmed his finger over the seam of her sex, pressing so lightly he didn't penetrate. "She wants to."

Her toes curled. She was so empty inside, it ached.

He slid up and around her clit and wiggled the hood. "She doesn't want to." Down again. "She wants to." Up. "She doesn't want to."

As he slid toward her bottom again, she whined, "Please, Sir. Please. I can't hold still."

"What do you need?"

"May I please come, Sir?"

"I thought you'd never ask." He settled himself between her thighs and followed the crease of her thigh with the tip of his tongue, circled her clit, and followed the path to her other thigh. She sucked in a breath, and her stomach muscles quivered. After his soft foreplay, she didn't expect him to dive in, so when he used his fingers to peel back her labia and sucked her clit into his mouth with insistent pulls, she let out a little scream.

She curled her hands around the ropes binding her to the headboard. Needing the anchor, she cherished the safety the hold provided her.

Against Charlotte's will, her hips began to undulate, but Master used his forearms on her upper legs to pin her to the bed, all the while keeping her open and exposed with his fingers. She strained against his hold and against the impending orgasm, both wanting and fearing it.

She was hot all over, and her skin tingled with a fine sheen of perspiration. Her breast and nipples were so swollen that when she looked down her body, she could see them jump with her heartbeat. But what took her breath away was the smartly dressed, dark-haired man between her legs. She couldn't keep her head up as her muscles tensed, and her clitoris became even more sensitive.

As if he sensed her nearing the pinnacle, he slowed his ministration down, blood rushed in her ears, producing a roaring sound, her heart hammered, and she took in lungfuls of air as she approached the peak.

Her entire lower half was on fire, and then he lifted his head, ordered her, "Come for me," and blew air over her fully exposed clit.

She hit the precipice, and wave after wave of pleasurable contractions wracked her body as every bit of pent-up tension released. He blew again, and she shuddered as the sensation wrung more pleasurable aftershocks from her.

She sagged into the pillow as she caught her breath. Uncurling her hands from the bonds, she tried to remember the last time she had been this relaxed. For the moment, everything was right with the world. Later she could worry how Byron never failed to bring her to climax. The only man who'd managed to do so in years. A man who wasn't her husband. Although Liam had let his business partner use her for sex, she hadn't considered it adultery since he'd been the instigator and present. Moreover, she never enjoyed any of the extramarital activities before, but now...

The familiar, throaty warning sound jerked her out of her head and back into the present. Something slick but hard and unyielding pressed against her anus, and she groaned. Michael loved to fuck her in the ass, and his sodomy always hurt. She was also sure he liked it *because* it hurt her.

The pressure eased. "Color?"

Without realizing, she'd tensed against the intrusion and, observant as always, Sir noticed. She opened her mouth to call, "Red," but closed it again to think. "Yellow"—she stretched the word—"ish."

Her answer surprised a chuckle out of him. Mellowed by the orgasms, she also grinned and lifted her head from the pillow. "I don't enjoy anal like men seem to do."

His bear-sized hand stroked her thigh, and again it amazed her how gentle they could be. "Is it because you consider it to be taboo?"

"No... not really. It's just that..."

"It was painful?" he offered when she hesitated.

"Yes," she admitted.

"Anal can be painful if care isn't taken to prepare you first, but it can also be very stimulating. I will use ample lubrication and stretch you carefully. Can you trust me to do this without hurting you?"

Trust him—a man? Any man? The thought was ludicrous, but she did trust him. Sort of.

At least, enough to let him tie me to the bed.

Her gaze dropped to the object he held in his free hand.

And that plug doesn't look too large.

"Will you stop if I ask you?"

"Use red and everything stops."

"I trust you." She swallowed and lifted her chin. "Green, Sir."

His smile flashed as he circled a finger around her labia and slowly worked the plug inside. She gasped at the sensation. Somehow, the stimulation at her backside added to the pleasure his finger evoked, and with the liberal amount of lube, the plug slid home without any pain.

"I figured you might like the plug." Using his shoulder to nudge her thighs apart, he flattened his tongue and licked from the base of the anal toy all the way up to her pubic bone. Then he tilted his face so she got an excellent view of his smug satisfaction as he calmly stated, "For each orgasm, you'll get a bigger plug. I believe the set has five sizes."

She groaned and flopped her head back on the pillow.

13

DAY THIRTEEN

Waking up in a beam of sunlight, she twisted to her back, stretched, and bumped her shoulder against something solid and warm. She froze mid-stretch.

Was she back with Liam?

The blanket around her naked body was heavy and she took a shallow breath. Relief flooded her senses as she recognized the fresh scent of Byron instead of the heavy mix of alcohol, cigars, and deodorant which seemed to cling to Liam.

Lying as immobile as possible, she took stock of her body. Her asshole was a bit sore, that last plug had been very big after all, and her stomach muscles hurt from the many orgasms, but other than that, she felt amazing. She kept her breathing light as her thoughts traveled back to last night and how Byron used orgasm after orgasm to drive her out of her mind. The urge to kiss him and to return the favor made her skin tingle.

Would she dare to?

As slow as a chameleon approached a juicy cricket, she turned and took him in.

The bright sunlight made his scars stand out a bit more, but that didn't have her staring. Sometime during the night, the blanket had slid down and now revealed his powerful upper body with a smattering of hair on his chest and an enticing happy trail. The line drew her attention to the part of his body still concealed by the bedding. She looked at his face again. He appeared to be asleep, his features relaxed. Around his mouth interesting dark stubble formed a shadow, accentuating his sensual lips.

Her gaze fell on the covers again. She propped herself up on one elbow and carefully took hold of the blanket. She lifted the fabric from his hips and almost dropped the covers. From a neatly trimmed nest of curls an impressive morning wood stood at attention and saluted her.

A guy's package had never appealed to her, not even Liam's at the start of their relationship before his abuse took away every appeal he had. Now, this cock was a different story altogether and a thing of beauty. His girth was a bit more than she was used to, and his member was straight and smooth with pronounced veins. What made her swallow in awe was his length, the tip easily reaching his belly button.

She rose to her knees on the bed and shuffled toward him. The shaft was slightly darker than the rest of his body and the glans of the penis was smooth, engorged, and invited her to touch. On instinct, she bent and licked over the mushroom at the top. His erection bobbed, and encouraged, she ran her tongue down the long vein toward his ball sack.

A bear-sized hand curled in her long hair, and she froze.

"Good morning."

His raspy and sleepy voice shot straight between her legs, and she relaxed when she realized he wasn't angry or put off by her forwardness. Lifting her gaze, she met burning blue pools of lust without an ounce of sleepiness within them.

"Good morning, Sir." She couldn't contain her grin, no matter how hard she tried.

"Kittycat." His fingers tightened, in a subtle warning, before he loosened his grip. "What is it you're doing?"

Her relationship with Byron over the last two weeks had boosted her self-respect. Her lungs expanded to their fullest, and she decided to tease him a bit. "Right now, I'm waiting for you to release my hair so I can give you a proper morning blow job."

He arched an eyebrow, and her cheeks burned. When she tried to avert her gaze, his grip on her hair thwarted the attempt. "Don't go shy on me now, Kittycat. Tell me what you want."

"I want to taste this." Emboldened by his demand, with the tip of her finger she circled over the urethra slit and over the corona. Again, his erection bobbed and a pearl of precum gathered at the slit. She swept it up with her finger and brought the drop to her mouth. Darting out her tongue, she caught the liquid and swallowed.

The hand in her hair pulled, sending pinpricks of pain across her scalp. The sensation didn't frighten her or slow her down. She was driving him crazy and stealing his control and the knowledge emboldened her.

Fellatio never had been pleasant, but nothing sex-related with Liam had. The times Michael stuffed his dick in her mouth, she loathed the humiliation that came with gagging, loss of air, and something disgusting spurting in the back of her throat. She wanted to replace those memories with giving head to a man who gave more than he took. A man who was careful and controlled in his dominance. This time she wanted to do this out of free will... and love.

Her throat thickened, but before she could dwell on her last thought, Byron pulled her on top of him.

His hand brushed over her head and settled on the back of her neck.

For a moment time stood still as they stared into each other's eyes. Their bond intensified as if some invisible rope bound them together and made them more connected. Her gaze dropped to his lips. She was sure they would connect in the literal sense of the word soon, but right now they were connected on an emotional level she'd never experienced before.

He trailed his fingertips over her cheek. "You feel it too, don't you?"

She nodded, unable to form the words.

He pressed a soft kiss on her lips and kept his smoldering gaze locked with hers. Almost like he was savoring the moment, he took her mouth in a slow and seductive rhythm.

Her eyes fluttered closed as the warmth built in her heart. He tasted of mint and man, his lips firm but soft and a little dry. She wanted more, didn't want him to hold back. Charlotte pushed the tip of her tongue between her lips and touched his bottom lip. He opened at her silent request, and she slid the tip of her tongue into his mouth.

Their hands roamed and their breathing became uneven as they stoked their passion. Charlotte rubbed her breasts against his chest and enjoyed the tickle of the coarse hair.

Byron was still on his back with her half on top

of him, and though she didn't completely control the kiss, for the moment she was more in control than ever before with him.

She enjoyed and even craved his dominance and wondered when the leash he had on his inner caveman would snap. She stilled mid-kiss and gently took his lower lip between her teeth and pulled it slowly back. For a moment nothing happened, and she teased the tip of her tongue over the extended flesh.

His control shook and snapped free.

The next moment, Charlotte was on her back, Byron looming over her.

He bracketed her face between his palms and kissed her, his tongue dipping in. She moaned and arched as his tongue made wet trails over her puckered lips.

Her heart started to race, but not in fear.

Byron pulled back. Impossible long lashes fluttered against flushed skin, and her lips were pink and swollen from his kisses. She was in one word… gorgeous. But what had his mind reeling was her courage and generosity. Which reminded him… "I guess I should let you have your wicked way with me then, hmm?" His voice came out hoarse as he pushed himself back and rolled.

She blinked as if to clear away the fog in her mind.

Giving her a moment, he fisted his cock and ran his hand from the base to the head. He stroked himself a few times, and her eyes followed the movement as she propped up on one elbow.

"Let's set some ground rules, okay?" He waited for her to nod before he continued, "I like to have control and while I'm prepared to give you free rein for now, I might take over somewhere in the process. The moment you want me to stop, tap my leg twice."

Something vulnerable flashed on her face, then it was gone, and she looked him straight in his face. "I will." A pause. "Thank you, Sir."

He released his length and curled his fists in the blanket. "When I'm ready to come, I will tap you on the shoulder. You can decide if you want to pull back or not."

The relief and disbelief in her expression were equally gut-wrenching.

Bloody, stupid, fucking incompetent bastard of a husband.

Willing the man from his thoughts, he focused on the woman kneeling up to him.

With trembling fingers, she reached out. He dropped his head onto the pillow and prayed this would be a positive experience for her. She lowered her head and nuzzled and kissed the length of him. Byron groaned.

Fuck me, I can't imagine how it must feel when she takes me in her mouth.

With the strangest mix of sensations, his body stiffened and relaxed at the same time. He heaved air into his lungs, inhaling a whiff of Bvlgari Thé Bleu and the heady scent of their mixed arousal.

She swirled her tongue around the tip, rubbing against the sensitive underside of the ridge, almost shredding his resolve, and he fisted the blankets more tightly.

She opened her mouth wider and licked, nipped, and kissed her way down to his balls. Testing his determination, she teased his sack with soft lips and a lashing tongue. He closed his eyes and concentrated on the feelings. Working her way back up to the tip, she used the same soft teasing touches, and it drove him crazy. Then his eyes flew open when she drew him into her mouth.

He grunted. "That's it. Just like that. Jesus, Kittycat."

Sucking up his praise, she bobbed her head faster. Another low groan escaped from his throat, and his legs trembled. Engulfed in her warm, wet heat for mere minutes, his balls were already drawing up. She sucked the head of his cock inside, and her tongue wiggled against the sensitive underside. Without a conscious thought, his fingers found her hair.

He pressed his backside into the mattress, to prevent his pelvis from thrusting forward. It was far too soon to take over. Another guttural sound escaped him. She was reducing him to a caveman. He pulled on her hair, forcing his cock in further.

"That's it, Kittycat, tighten the suction of your mouth when you draw up. Flatten your tongue and take me deeper. Aghh." His legs shook as he strained against the instinctive need to thrust his hips. "Lick under the head and wiggle your tongue. Yes, just like that. Use your hand as a counterpoint and twist your wrist." Another groan escaped him. "Holy hell, kitten!"

He'd had his fair share of blow jobs, some good, some mediocre, some excellent, but none of them compared to this experience. A tingling up his spine warned him of his impending orgasm and he tapped her shoulder. Her grip around the base of his dick tightened and she bobbed at a faster pace, never losing her rhythm. Then her other hand found his balls and fondled them.

"Kitten!" He shouted and shoved his cock deep. She spluttered and swallowed, the contraction of her throat strangling his cock and spurring on his climax. Over and over, he pulsed in her mouth. He gentled his hold on her hair and he flattened against the bed, his breaths wheezing in and out. Little aftershocks sizzled through him as she licked and suckled him clean with the sweetest submission and care. If he hadn't been half in love with her already, this might seal the deal.

This woman is mine!

"Thank you, Kittycat." He bent down and kissed her, not minding the taste of himself on her tongue as he took the kiss deeper.

DAY FOURTEEN

"Come here, Kittycat." After disconnecting the conference call, Master pushed away from the computer and patted his thigh.

Taking a deep breath, she ignored the warmth radiating through her body and walked to him. His approving smile softened his hard features, and when she climbed on his lap without prompting, he wrapped his arms around her and murmured a "good girl" in her hair.

She exhaled slowly and relaxed against his chest. For a moment they didn't talk but just sat, enjoying each other, and after a while, Charlotte realized she was synchronizing her breathing with his, in the same way she adjusted her footsteps with a person she walked with, or mirrored a friend's posture during a conversation.

The sense of being connected to him on a

profound and intimate level was overwhelming but exhilarating. He seemed to feel the connection as well and appeared content with holding her like this.

He's such an amazing man—caring and controlled, and I don't mind his bossiness.

When he leaned back and kissed her temple, she felt a bit sad and tried to get up. His arms around her tightened in a silent warning and reproval. "Don't move, kitten." He shifted her in his arms, so they could see each other's face. "I want to talk about some things you might find hard, and I think you'll need the comfort of my arms."

"Oh." Despite her effort to stay relaxed, she stiffened, and from the knowing smirk, he hadn't missed her struggle. She sighed. "Okay, what is it you want to discuss?"

"Such a disgruntled face." He chuckled, and her heart lifted as his eyes lightened with humor.

I'm happier, but he seems more contented, too.

She tried to school her features, but he rubbed his nose with hers in a sweet and playful gesture. "Don't hide your feelings. I prefer it when you communicate openly and honestly with me."

"Oh, okay." She dropped her head, and her voice reached barely above a whisper.

He tipped her head back up with an insistent finger under her chin. "What did I just say about hiding?"

"Sorry."

He blinked reassuringly.

Relief flooded her. "I'm not sure why I hide or worry I'll displease you. My mind knows you won't lash out in anger, but…" her sentence dried up in her throat and she chewed her bottom lip.

He hummed. "It's what you've been conditioned to do and to expect." With a fingertip, he pulled the flesh she was worrying from between her teeth. "Keep your eyes on me, kitten."

He waited until she lifted her head.

When did I drop my gaze again?

"Excellent." He gave her a firm nod. "This is exactly why I want you on my lap. We're going to practice sharing our thoughts and emotions." His teeth flashed and the lines beside his eyes crinkled. "There's that expression again."

She grinned too and ruefully shook her head. Hyperaware of his every move, she slid her hand down his arm and laced her fingers with his.

His much larger hand squeezed hers and he curled his other arm more securely around her back. "I'll start and then I expect you to share." He dipped his head and gave her a level look.

"Yes, Sir." A different answer was simply out of the question.

He gave her a firm nod. "I was pleasantly surprised when I caught you checking me out, yesterday."

A giggle escaped her, and she slapped her free hand over her mouth.

"Now, that's a lovely sound. I totally intend to have you giggling some more before I let you off my lap." The grin he sent her way was so wicked, she almost choked on her saliva. After slapping her back a few times and making sure she was all right, he continued "My days have been wonderful with you, and to have you offering a blow job? Kittycat, you blew more than my dick."

She giggled more and didn't attempt to stifle the sound.

"The sensation of your wet hot mouth around my cock was so erotic, I was afraid I would come within seconds when you engulfed me with your lips and rubbed your tongue along the crown."

A tingling swept up the back of her neck and crept across her face.

Great, I'm blushing like a teenager again.

She swallowed a few times but couldn't get rid of the lump in her throat. Light-headed, she stared at their tangled hands, before she remembered he wanted to see her reactions.

She forced herself to make eye contact. "It–it embarrasses me to think how brazen I was." She let her gaze drop, caught herself when he made the low warning sound in the back of his throat, and snapped her head back up.

"Go on," he prompted.

My goodness, why is this so hard?

"I also think, and I know this is going to sound absolutely ridiculous, but I feel like I'm being disloyal to Liam."

Master hummed and played with her fingers. It was just enough distraction for her to be able to continue.

"My marriage is dead, has been dead for a long time." She shook her head. "I don't even know if the relationship with Liam ever stood a chance." Scowling she muttered, "I still don't know why Liam wanted to marry me. I've never really believed he even liked me very much."

He leaned in and stroked his sensual mouth over her downturned lips. She stared into searing, intelligent eyes.

He broke the kiss far too soon to her liking. "And that makes you feel…"

"Unwanted, unattractive, in the way." Her eyes widened when her words sank in.

Did I just say that out loud? How mortifying!

Almost as a reward for her honesty, he trailed open-mouth kisses along the underside of her jaw until he reached her neck where he suckled and licked at the spot that made her legs tremble as she clung to his shoulders.

All thoughts about her marriage and her assumptions about good and bad flew out the window. In this penthouse and the world of Byron

Nolan, there was no place for black and white. This world consisted of incredibly bright, flamboyant colors. And every single day she fell a little bit more for this incredible man.

Deciding to be brave, she whispered, "I love you."

He stilled and groaned against her skin. "Say it again."

"I love you." Her voice was firmer now.

"Fuck, woman." He squeezed her so hard, he just might have cracked a few ribs, but she didn't protest. Especially not when he followed with, "I love you, too."

Wanting to jump up and down with the elation his words elicited, she settled for curling her hand around his nape and pulling him in for a kiss. For a few of her hammering heartbeats, he let her control the kiss before he took over, dominating her mouth, mastering her body, captivating her mind.

My goodness, never in my life have I been kissed so passionately.

He took her mouth deep and hot, his hand around her jaw angling her head in every way he wanted. But she gave him her all in return. Their tongues tangled, pushed, and prodded before retreating and luring the other into the play.

Eventually, clearly reluctantly, he pulled back. After giving her a light kiss, he set her on her feet. "Although I'd enjoy holding you longer, we both have work to do. And I'm liable to strip you naked and have my way with you on my desk. I have had some very carnal dreams about you and this desk."

Glancing at the table, she squeezed her legs together against the ache in her core. His words and the visual of being spread out over the desk and ravaged made moving impossible. "Um, I, Um."

Again, her attention slid to the desk, and she didn't move away. Byron couldn't tear his gaze from her.

I shouldn't.

Byron clenched and unclenched his fists. Raw need sparked inside him, and without a conscious decision, he let go of his control. The next moment, he scooped her up and reveled in the little squeak of surprise. What made his heart soar, was how she wrapped her legs around his waist and clung to his shoulders.

Holding her against his chest with one arm, he swiped every item off his desk with the other. He lowered her to the flat surface and stole a kiss. A giggle escaped her and shot straight to his groin.

"Woman," he growled, "you drive me out of my mind. With that sexy little body, you are perfect in today's outfit."

He raked his eyes over her. The black petticoat under the mini dress teased the tops of long white stockings with enticing bows and had driven him crazy with lust all morning. The red corset dress pushed up her small breasts and the red of the hood contrasted beautifully with her golden blonde hair. "It makes me truly feel like the big bad wolf."

Her eyes sparkled with mischief. "Oh, Grandmother, what large ears you have."

He caught on and played along. "All the better to hear you with."

"Oh, Grandmother, what large eyes you have."

"All the better to see you with."

"Oh, Grandmother, what a large mouth you have."

"All the better to eat you with." He nudged her ankle. "Open for me," he ordered, not caring the least how deep and gruff the words came out. Apparently, neither did she.

His Kittycat parted her legs and revealed the wet swatch of fabric covering her pussy. He dove between her thighs and nuzzled the crease between her leg and crotch. She smelled divine–clean and musky with a hint of lavender.

"You won't be needing these," he all but growled and ripped the flimsy material at the seams. She bucked and he anchored her to the desk with his hands splayed above the innocent, but sexy white stockings.

He cradled her hips and ran his nose over her slit. Continuing the up and down movement of his face between her legs, he circled his index fingers over and around the protruding hipbones. She tried to wiggle away, but he dug in his thumbs in a warning and lifted his head. "Don't move."

He teased his fingers even lighter over her sensitized skin. Giggles erupted from her, and again she strained against his hold. "Please. Don't. Stop, that tickles!"

Diverting her, he ran his tongue over the seam of her sex and enjoyed the burst of the tangy and musky flavor. She was already creaming, and he took his time to lap it all up. Resting his lips over her clit, he danced his fingers over her hips again.

"Oh, my goodness." She gasped, belly laughed, and struggled to prop herself up on her elbows. "Stop! Please."

He grinned against her mound and sucked on the swelling pearl. Her hips bucked as wild as a bronco bursting from the chute, and he hung on like a rodeo rider. Enjoying her responses, Byron lifted his head, caught her eyes, and held her trapped in his gaze.

He drew three circles clockwise, counterclockwise, and back, and gave a stinging nip to the inside of her thigh. She squealed, and he licked the tiny bite with the tip of his tongue. Curling his hands, he scraped his fingernails over her hipbones. She exploded in uncontrollable laughter and reflexively slammed her legs together violently enough to make his ears ring. He loved her responses!

Returning to a reassuring hold on her hips, he waited for her to ease her thighs open again.

The moment she realized what she was doing, her legs fell apart. "I'm so sorry. Did I hurt you?"

He chuckled. "Stop fretting. You didn't hurt me, and you have a beautiful laugh."

"Oh, my goodness, you're evil. Do you know that?"

"Sometimes," he agreed unapologetically. Making her laugh was as gratifying as making her come.

Guess what's next on my agenda!

DAY FIFTEEN

The following morning, Charlotte woke up cranky and irritated without knowing the real cause. Her mood did an even bigger nosedive when she spotted the clothing for today: a black leather corset, a tiny thong, and no shoes.

She placed her hands on her hips and scowled at the innocent corset with lacing at the back.

How the hell am I going to get into you on my own? And why does he want me in something like this? A corset might be gorgeous on a woman with an hourglass figure. I'm more a... stick.

She stared down at her naked body. Actually, now that she was less stressed, and Master took care of her and made sure she ate healthy meals, she was filling out.

Her thoughts came to a screeching halt. In the

exact same way a corset molded a person's figure, Byron Nolan was molding her. Her temper rose. He might not be as cruel and callous as Liam and Michael, but he was manipulating her. Or wasn't he?

Her thoughts muddled and she sank on the bed beside the corset. The mattress dipped and the thong slid to the floor. She didn't care. Charlotte scuttled back and pulled up her knees. With her arms around her shins, she rested her chin on her bent legs and tried to think.

She was still in the same position and her mind was equally stuck when Master came looking for her at a quarter past eight.

"Kittycat?" Worry made his voice drop an octave. "What's the matter? Is something wrong? Are you all right?"

"Uhuh." The sound she made was neither a confirmation nor a rebuttal. Truth be told, she didn't understand what was wrong with her today.

He crossed the room and pressed his hand against her forehead.

She twisted away from him and snapped, "I don't have a fever."

His brows knitted together, and his beautiful eyes darkened, but Charlotte wasn't in a mood to be considerate, to practice restraint, or to heed self-preservation. "Just leave me alone."

"Excuse me?" Iron fingers gripped her chin.

She blinked and helplessly stared up into his face.

No, I am not helpless!

She released the hold on her legs and shackled his wrists.

His jaw flexed and he dropped his eyes to her hands. "Let go, kitten. Lace your hands behind your head."

"No."

His mouth tightened, and his face grew colder than she thought possible. Gone was the indulgent lover and the caring Master, this was the ruthless businessman, who acquired and dismantled companies, fired people, and bought women for his enjoyment.

Her anger kept escalating, and her blood roared in her ears like a fire. It burned a path through her body and into her soul, eating and licking everything in its way.

He said something, but she couldn't hear him above the all-consuming rage.

Somehow, he broke her hold on his wrists and took her by the shoulders. Gave her a gentle shake. "Charlotte! Do. You. Need. Your. Safeword?"

Safeword?

Uncomprehending, she blinked and tried to get her head straight.

What's happening to me?

She shook her head, not in denial but to clear her mind. The fog didn't want to recede.

"Charlotte."

Why isn't he calling me Kittycat? And why are my cheeks wet?

He hoisted her from the bed, reversed their positions, and sat down with her perched on his thighs.

She didn't want to be on his lap, did she?

But her hands curled around the lapels of his suit jacket, and she snuggled her face in the crook of his neck. Shame and confusion washed over her, but when she opened her mouth to apologize, nothing came out.

He stroked her hair. "I think you're experiencing subdrop. How long have you been unsettled like this? What did I miss?"

She sniffled, hiccupped, and forced herself to meet his eyes. "I'm not sure. I woke up like this, I think."

He hummed and kept stroking her hair. She liked the touch and leaned in.

"Okay, so you were out of sorts when you woke. Were you thinking about something in particular or did you wake from a dream that upset you?"

She chewed her lip, and he used the pad of his thumb to carefully remove the flesh from between her teeth.

"I don't think so. I was just… unhappy, I guess, but not for a reason."

"Okay, what happened next?"

"I did my morning routine." She frowned at her fists, still clutching the dark fabric of his jacket.

I should loosen my hold.

She couldn't. "I don't think that changed something, but when I saw today's clothing, I went from cranky to angry."

"Why?"

"I don't like the corset."

His expression didn't change, but his hand shifted to her cheek. "Explain." With the lightest pressure, he made her face him again.

She stiffened.

Bare her soul? Share her vulnerabilities? Vulnerabilities he could exploit.

She toyed with a loose thread on the edge of her towel and couldn't form the words.

"Kittycat." The rumbling growled nickname sent a shot of pleasure and a frisson of fear over her spine.

"I don't know how to put it on." Her answer was true and not evasive… quite.

"I figured as much." Master sighed. "I was expecting to strap you in myself. However, I didn't expect I was required to fetch you, or that you wouldn't be dressed at all."

"Oh, right." Totally inadequate reaction. "Yes,

yes, of course. I'm sorry." One hundred percent the truth.

His index finger tapped her cheek lightly. "Now tell me what else bothers you."

"Um, n-nothing."

Such a bloody liar!

He didn't speak.

Charlotte let her gaze drop to her lap, and he made the throaty sound that told her she screwed up.

"Keep your eyes on me and answer my question." There was a hint of steel in his tone, but —to her relief— he didn't seem mad. "I suggest you go for a truthful one this time."

She took in a deep breath and rushed out on a long exhalation. "I don't think I have the figure for a corset."

He blinked. "Why not?"

She gestured an impatient hand over her body. "Don't you need breasts for a corset? A waist? Some thighs? Doesn't work on a stick, I think." The last words came out far more sarcastically than she intended, and she flinched and braced herself.

Master heaved a sigh. "I don't even know where I should begin to address the nonsense that's currently coming out of your mouth, so I'll do them chronologically. One, you have breasts. They are gorgeous and perky, are tipped with the most beautiful and responsive nipples, and fit in my hands like a pair of doves."

She blinked and stared open-mouthed at him. He seemed absolutely honest and sincere.

"Two, you have a waist. Are you aware how much I enjoy the way my hands can span completely around your middle and how I love to hold you tight and secure?"

Her heart stuttered at the conviction in his face and in his voice. She shook her head in wordless wonder.

"Three, true, you could use some padding on your thighs, but on a healthy meal plan, enough sleep, and less stress you're already filling out a bit. Besides, even with your hipbones protruding from your body, the center between those thighs contains so much warm softness, I couldn't care less."

She gasped at his carnal bluntness, he chuckled and lifted a shoulder in a casual "so sue me" motion.

"For the remark about being a stick, I should paddle your ass with one. A stick is a dead piece of wood and you're very much alive. Where wood has no give, you yield beautifully to my commands and my touch."

Heat singed her cheeks.

"That sums up what you said. Now, let me address the matter of how you spoke to me and make it a list again. One"—he held up his index finger between them—"you don't talk bad about my kitten. Two, you don't snap at me." He lifted a second finger. "And—finally—three, sarcasm doesn't suit you. At all."

Charlotte concentrated on his hand and blinked hard. He was right. "I'm sorry, Sir." She gulped. "I have absolutely no idea what's the matter with me today."

"Ah, Kittycat, come here." He pulled her against his chest and cradled her as tenderly as one would an upset child.

A tear trickled in a wet trail over her cheek. She let out a sob. More tears followed, and then she was crying in earnest.

All the time, Master held her on his lap and shifted backward during her crying fit until he leaned against the headboard. A low comforting sound rumbled beneath her ear and, as she quieted, Charlotte realized he was humming *The Rose* from Bette Midler. While she listened to the familiar tune, she rested her head beneath his chin, and for this moment, her world was right again.

DAY SIXTEEN

"You want what?" She cringed at the sharp accusation in her voice, and quickly lowered her face but
tracked his movements through her eyelashes.

Always be aware of the possibly angry man, right?

She whispered a hasty, "Sorry, Sir," just to be
sure.

He gave her an indulgent smile but didn't make a
move. His posture was relaxed. He'd shoved his
right hand in his trouser pocket earlier and didn't
pull it out. His left arm hung loosely, fingers
pointing down. She perused the rest of his body
upwards until their eyes met. He wore a "panic if
you must" expression, which might have been
condescending, if not for the warmth in his eyes.

All right. She exhaled through pursed lips and let
go of the fight or flight rigidity the adrenaline
coursing through her body pumped into her

muscles. Getting her pounding heart under control would take a bit longer, she guessed.

The scar beside his sparkling eyes deepened and the corners of his mouth curled. "Unless you call out 'red' right now, I'm going to flog you."

Instead of frightening her like the first time he mentioned his intention, his statement now relaxed her. It took her a moment to understand why.

Because he gave me a safeword and just reminded me I'm in control, even when bound, but still...

"Why do you want to hurt me?"

Now he did move closer, but he didn't touch her. His energy, however, caressed her skin and made her hormones go into overdrive.

Great, now my heart is drumming against my ribcage for another reason.

"I'm not going to hurt you, Kittycat. Any flogger can hurt, but when used with care, they feel more like a massage."

Uhuh.

He chuckled. "Look at that pout. Do you really have such little faith in me?"

She canted her head, so her hair hid her burning cheeks.

A careful finger tipped her face back up to him. "Can you trust me to do this and not hurt you, or do you need your safeword?"

"I trust you." The words rushed from her mouth. "It's just..."

He considered her. "You're not afraid of the pain, but afraid I'd like to hurt you, is that it?"

Her shoulders sagged.

How does he know me so well?

"Yes," she whispered, "that's exactly it."

He pulled her stiff body against him, and her arms snaked around his middle.

Resting her head against his chest, she allowed the slow lub-dub of his heartbeat, his fresh scent, and his warm body to comfort and relax her.

She couldn't tell how long they stood like that, but when she finally pulled back, her body had stopped shaking, and her heart rate had slowed to a slow jog instead of a full-out sprint rhythm.

Without giving herself time to think the better of it, she grasped his hand and started to pull him to the bedrooms.

He bellowed a laugh and followed her.

When they reached his bedroom, he took over. With his free hand he opened the door, with the other still holding hers, he guided her toward the four-poster bed. Now she noticed the bolts embedded in the posts.

He let go of her hand and pressed a kiss to her shoulder. "I'm proud of you, kitten. Take off your clothes and place them on the bed, please."

While she undressed and neatly folded her clothes, he rummaged through an antique wooden chest and produced two fleece-lined leather cuffs,

short chains, and a multi-stranded whip. A whip.
She shuddered.

I trust him, but…

She bit her lip. "You'll stop when I say red?"

"Absolutely." He tossed the items on the bed and
cupped her cheek. "But I'm also going to check with
you often to see how you're doing. How's this, we're
going to use a scale from one to ten, where one is
no pain and ten is excruciating."

She nodded. "I know the system; they use it in
hospitals." She bit her lip as she remembered vividly
how she knew the practice.

He made his throaty warning sound. "There's no
place for him in our bedroom."

"I know. I'm sorry."

The scars creased. "Don't be. The ugly memories
will fade." He tilted his head. "Ready?"

Without speaking, she held out her wrists. He
buckled the leather cuffs around them and pressed a
kiss to each palm. "I'm honored by your trust."

He used the chains to restrain her between the
posts. She faced the bed with her arms in a high V.
Pity she wasn't feeling like cheering in victory but
more like begging for mercy.

Her breathing hitched as she pulled on the
chains.

*Tied and helpless with a man, who was going to whip
her. Was she insane?*

"I-I…" What did she want to say?

Even as she tried to figure out what to say, excitement mixed with her fear.

How can I get turned on, even if I'm scared spitless?

A masculine chuckle made her jump a little. "Did I say that out loud?"

He stroked her hair over her shoulders to her front. "Hmhm, you did."

His hands ventured lower, and he trailed his fingertips over her collarbone and the tops of her breasts. "Remember, I don't plan to go over a four or five on the pain scale, and the flogger won't leave any bruising. If anything lingers, it will resemble a light sunburn and disappear within a few hours."

"That's reassuring, thank you for telling me, Sir."

Strong but careful fingers gripped her chin, and he turned her face for a deep, lingering kiss. By the time he pulled back, she was a puddle of goo and wouldn't have batted an eyelash if he pulled out a bullwhip.

She leaned her head against her outstretched arm.

With firm hands, he stroked her arms, her back, massaged her buttocks, and stroked down her legs. Snug leather cuffs closed around her ankles, and she couldn't suppress a whimper. He stilled and stroked her calves. "Color?"

She looked over her shoulder. He was kneeling behind her. "Your leg!"

His smile was warm. "Don't worry, sweetheart,

the damage to my leg is done and kneeling doesn't hurt." His lips curled further up. "Just don't expect to see me on my knees before you often."

She choked on a laugh. "I can't believe you can make me laugh right now, but you did, and I'm at green again. Please continue, Sir. I don't want to live my life as a frightened rabbit."

"Brave Kittycat."

The chains jangled as he secured her legs to the underside of the bedposts.

The sound was ominous, but his hands caressing her outer thighs kept her anchored and her fear at bay.

"I like to have you open for me, to watch how you surrender to me, and how you're going to accept the kiss of the flogger."

The fabric of his dress shirt stroked her buttocks and back as he rose and pressed his muscled chest against her.

When he cupped her shoulders and pushed closer to her, the distinctive ridge of his erection pressed against her backside, and heat sizzled through her body, distracting her from her worries.

With firm strokes, he rubbed his hands over her shoulders and arms, up again and down her back, ass, and thighs. Each stroke wakened her skin, settled her anxiety, and ignited her libido. Pressing his front against her back again, he reached around her, stroked her belly, and teased the tickle spot at her hips, making her giggle and squirm in her bonds.

When he moved his hands upwards, palmed her breasts, and teased and rolled her nipples, her squirming was for a different reason and slickness coated her folds and thighs.

His hand slipped higher, and he sucked on her earlobe. She relaxed, lowered her eyelids, and parted her lips on a soft sigh.

Using one hand, he encircled her throat. Trembling, she sucked in a breath. He didn't use any pressure, just held his hand around her air supply. The gesture was possessive and dominant, but it didn't frighten her.

Master will take care of me, and I can relax in his care.

The revelation was so freeing. Releasing the breath she was holding, she gave over the reins completely. Engulfed by his warmth, his strength, and breathing in his scent, she leaned against him.

"You're such a good girl," he whispered in her ear and stepped away. Before she could miss his heat and comfort, velvety fingers tickled over her back. He caressed the skin with the flogger before the strands left her body and returned with a strange sensation.

She let out a small gasp at the shock, but it didn't hurt—not even a sting.

"Can you give me a number?" His hand pressed against the flogged skin, and heat sizzled inside her.

"About a two, Sir."

"Excellent." He moved the strands up and down her back in a careful rhythm.

She swayed like leaves in the wind with the impact and allowed herself to drift. The strokes went over her buttocks to her thighs and back up. Her bottom, thighs, and back began to sting, and the blows left a light burning sensation behind.

The moment, she reached the point of discomfort, he eased off and stroked a cool hand over the burning flesh. Again, he inquired how she was doing.

She exhaled and swayed in her bindings. "About a five, Sir."

Is he done?

Without warning, he flicked strands over her left breast, and her eyes flew open.

Involuntarily, she pulled on the chains. She focused on his face. He wasn't looking at her breasts. He was studying her, running his eyes over her face, shoulders, and arms. Checking how she was doing.

His cheek creased and pulled on the scar. "Where are we on the scale?"

Scale? Oh, the pain scale.

"I think about a six."

He nodded and dropped the flogger on the bed.

A little dizzy, she allowed the chains to support her.

She inhaled sharply as his hand cupped her pussy. Her eyes rolled back in her head when he slid his hand between her legs. With his other hand on her buttocks, he held her in place. Even if she wanted to move, she couldn't. She moaned as he ran his finger around the slit and touched as if he had the right.

She shook with anticipation when he circled her clit with a barely-there touch and teased the hood. The need inside her expanded, but she couldn't move. Couldn't urge him on. Being helpless and bound only increased the heat. "Oh, my goodness."

Warm air puffed against her swollen tissues, and it was the only warning she got before he sucked her clit into his mouth.

Her clit hardened like a mini cock and every muscle in her lower half tightened like a coil. Her hips jerked, goosebumps raised on her skin, and her toes curled in the plush carpet. She trembled.

He drove her up and up, and as her insides bunched and readied for release, she sucked in a breath and held it. His tongue wiggled the hood, and the tight rein on her climax snapped like a frayed line. She cried out as her release rushed over her in wave after wave of pleasure.

As her breathing slowed, he eased her down by

nuzzling her thighs and licking the cream from her nether lips.

"Let me get you down, Kittycat," he murmured.

She just nodded and drifted on the aftermath of pleasure. She was vaguely aware he released her arms and helped her lean on the bed. She pressed her wobbling knees against the mattress, not trusting her legs to keep her up. Chains clanged, and her legs were free. He wrapped a soft blanket around her.

And he half dragged, half carried her further onto the mattress. She tried to help, but with a boneless body and the blanket in the way, she got nowhere.

"Settle, kitten, I've got you." He turned her and pulled her in a half-reclined position against his chest. She let her head drop back and inhaled his delicious scent.

She rubbed her cheek against the soft material of his dress shirt and played with the buttons. Her mind was still hazy, but she enjoyed lying half sprawled on top of him—liked the intimacy and the proximity.

"How did you like the flogger?"

His sexy voice rumbled in his chest, and she wanted to stay where she was and listen to him for the rest of her life.

"Kitten?"

"Um." She frowned and tried to remember his

question. Oh, the flogger. "I… I. You know, at first it scared me. I mean when I saw it first, I thought it looked horrible. I wasn't too sure about you using it on me."

He nodded and squeezed her against him. "Go on."

She narrowed her eyes at him. "Bossy much?"

"Yup." He grinned unrepentantly. "I'm a Dom, so get used to it. Now, quit stalling because I sense there's more."

She sighed and agreed. "There is. Okay, so I was nervous but when we talked, and you reminded me of the safeword and explained the intensity with a pain scale, the worry faded."

"Good to know." He kissed the top of her head and rested his chin on her hair. "So that was before we started. How do you feel about the actual flogging?"

She considered his question. Talking against his chest, she admitted "I liked it."

No, that's a lame answer.

"I didn't think I would, but you… well, when you stroked my skin, I became warm and aware of you and my own body. When you trailed the strands over me, it tickled." She wiggled her head until he lifted his chin, and she could look him in the face. "A nice tickle, mind you, not the nasty 'it makes me giggle so hard I might pee torture'."

His teeth flashed in a wide grin and his eyes gleamed wickedly.

He was so handsome it made her eyes hurt. "Why do you have to be so gorgeous?"

His expression sobered. "Kittycat, I'm scarred and could give small children nightmares."

"Not true. Especially not when those children would get to know you." She reached out and traced the deep pink lines carved in his flesh. "Will you tell me what caused these?"

He turned his head and pressed a kiss to her wrist. "Maybe someday but not now."

"Okay." A twinge of disappointment made her chest ache.

"I'm not brushing you off, kitten. It's just a long ugly story and right now I want to focus on your experience and not my scarred-up ugly mug."

"Ugly?" She slapped her palm on his chest and winced. Was he made out of concrete? "You remind me of an old French movie my nana liked. The main character Geoffrey is scarred too, but he is still a beautiful man. A line on his face can't diminish that, and neither can it for you."

His lips curled up, but the smile didn't reach his eyes. "Let's agree to disagree on this."

She hesitated, wanted to push past this strange insecurity from an otherwise utterly confident man. But they would have time, and right now she would do anything to erase the sadness, even by talking about embarrassing stuff.

She cleared her throat. "The flogger never really hurt, just burned a bit, and… it also turned me on." She cleared her throat again. Her mouth was bone dry.

With one arm curled securely around her, he took a sports drink from his nightstand and used his teeth to pull the cap. "Have a drink." He held the bottle in front of her and waited until she had a firm hold. She drank some of the liquid and lowered the bottle to her lap.

"Take a bit more."

She yawned and shook her head. "Too tired."

"A few more sips and then you can rest." He guided the bottle to her lips and held the bottle there until she finished almost half.

"Huh"—she blinked—"I guess I was thirsty after all."

He hummed. "Our brain isn't good at detecting thirst at the best of times. Since you went pretty deep into subspace, your mind is sluggish at best. Now rest or sleep." He took the bottle from her, placed it back on the nightstand, and pulled her snug against him. "I'll hold you."

She encircled his waist and clung to him because she wanted to hold him too.

DAY SEVENTEEN

"How are your back and thighs today?" Master glanced over the rim of his coffee cup.

"Fine, actually." She smiled at his scowl at her use of the word fine. "No, honestly. No lingering pain, and no marks or bruising. Only a pleasant soreness like after a vigorous workout."

Without a word, he held out his hand, and she rushed to join him. In the now familiar way, he tugged her onto his lap, and she snuggled against his chest. Inhaling his scent, touching his warm skin —even through his dress shirt, and listening to the steady beat of his heart never failed to make her feel comfortable and safe.

He rested his chin on her hair and let her enjoy the safety of his arms for long seconds.

When the weight of his head left, she tipped back her face and looked up at him.

"I wanted to go shopping with you for some vanilla wardrobe. Are you up for a trip to Zona Rosa Town Center, or should I arrange for a personal shopper to come to the penthouse?"

Charlotte wrinkled her forehead. In fact, she was ready for a trip, but she wasn't too keen on him spending more money on her.

"What?"

"You know me too well." She tried to scowl at him. "How is it possible after such a short amount of time?"

Master gripped her chin between thumb and forefinger. "Yes, I do. I know you well enough, to realize you're evading my question. Spill it, Kittycat. What is bothering you?"

Darn it.

Realizing she couldn't avert her gaze, she stilled. When he was both tender and domineering, she found him irresistible. "I think I would like to go outside for a while today." She hesitated, and then admitted, "I'm just not comfortable with you spending so much money on me." She tried to look down, but his hand tightened. Not enough to be painful, but enough to let her understand she wasn't supposed to look away. "Makes me feel cheap and greedy."

His foreboding mien morphed into something as close to tenderness as she'd ever witnessed from him. She swallowed.

"Kitten, I have more than enough money and I like spending it on you. Call me a possessive bastard, but I like the idea I've bought the fabric covering your beautiful body. The knowledge I paid for the swatch of lace and silk covering your breasts, ass and pussy"—he jerked up his hips and pressed a growing erection against her—"makes me hard every time."

He buried his face in her neck and licked and sucked at the hammering pulse point.

Caveman or not, his words and actions never failed to reduce her to a hot, lustful mess. She turned her face to the side and back, giving him as much access as possible.

Dressed comfortably in designer jeans and a light sweater, Charlotte admired the tall man beside her. Everything about him screamed confidence and control. He was cordial to her and everyone they met, but he commanded his surroundings without even trying. Where Liam's dominance came with a lot of posturing, threatening, and throwing his weight around, Byron didn't have to act the part. People took one look at his posture, stride, and the way he held his head and instinctively knew he wasn't a man who followed.

Charlotte also found the respect and deference

the people in the city paid him extended to her, and she was actually enjoying their outing.

Until Byron held open the door of yet another fashionable boutique, and she almost collided with a woman she recognized. Taking a leaf from Byron's book, Charlotte pulled her shoulders back and gave Kimberly a polite but distanced smile.

The unpleasant woman bit down on her lip, ignored her, and shot Byron a simpering look. Seriously?

Byron inclined his head but ignored the brunette. The woman was stunning, Charlotte had to give her that.

When Byron silently pulled Charlotte into his side and lifted her hand high enough to take over the bags containing their purchases from the last shop, Kimberly frowned. "I'm not sure what you see in her but"—she gave Charlotte a scaling glare–"I can totally see why she's with you."

Beside her, Byron stiffened at the comment, and Charlotte fought not to show how the remark hit home. She pushed out her chin. "Really?" She hoped her stare matched the other woman's in coldness. "Your comment is petty and uncalled for. You don't know me, and you have absolutely no clue about our relationship. Do yourself a service and get over yourself already. Envy is an ugly look and doesn't suit you."

She turned her attention to the man next to her.

"Come on, dear." She slid her hand into his and tangled their fingers together. "You wanted to look for shoes next, right?"

She almost giggled when Byron allowed her to lead him away, and she wondered who looked the most stunned of them—Kimberly or her Master.

They were about ten paces away from the green-eyed monster when Byron caught up with her and was back to his unflappable self.

"Whoa."

Okay, maybe still a little flapped. She giggled.

"Where did that come from? You were amazing."

Her chest swelled. "I was, wasn't I?"

"Yup." He pulled her into his arms and kissed the tip of her nose—not in the least embarrassed by the public display of affection. "I think I just fell even more in love with you."

DAY EIGHTEEN

"Can we go out for dinner tonight?"

Byron lifted an eyebrow at the completely unexpected question. Pride warmed his chest. He'd suspected their run-in with Kimberly would have set Charlotte back in her growth, but instead she seemed to have grown with the experience.

He pulled her onto his lap and nuzzled the juncture of her neck and shoulder. "Of course we can. What do you want to eat?"

She shrugged. "I don't really care. I just want some nice food, good wine, and to leave the penthouse for a while."

"You've been out yesterday," he reminded her—more to gauge her reaction than as a real objection.

She wrinkled her nose at him, and he pressed a kiss on the furrowed skin between her eyebrows.

"I just don't want to hide inside, and while

yesterday's encounter with Kimberly wasn't pleasant, I'm pleased it happened." She frowned. "Why are you smiling?"

He widened his eyes and schooled his features. "I'm not."

"You so are."

He wrapped his hand around her chin and anchored her in place. Then he closed the distance and kissed the pout of her lips.

* * *

"Have you given your future more thought?" Byron unfolded the napkin and placed it on his lap.

"Some." She traced the outline of her fork and chewed her bottom lip. "Aside from taking care of people and a household I don't have many skills, but maybe I can get a job cleaning or waitressing."

Leaning forward, Byron placed his palm over her restless fingers. "You have many more capabilities than you imagine. How about becoming a secretary?"

"What?" Her mouth fell open, and she snapped it shut as soon as she realized she must be as unattractive as a gaping fish.

Chuckling, he patted her hand. "Don't look so shocked, dear. You've been a great help for me."

"Uhuh."

He tilted his head and gave her a stern stare

from underneath his eyebrows. "You think I'm lying?"

She shrugged and gazed at the empty plate in front of her. At his signature admonishing sound, she looked up again.

"Better."

He nodded and his irises reminded her of the blue of a warm summer sky and cornflowers.

"Honesty and trust between a sub and her Dom are important, Kittycat. You've learned to trust me with your body. Can you trust me in this as well?"

Trust my Dom? But he's not mine, at least not past their month agreement.

"I do trust you. It's just..." she broke off mid-sentence, not sure how to continue.

He squeezed her fingers and let go of her hand when their server brought their starters. "Maybe your intellect trusts me to accept I'm telling the truth, but your self-doubt isn't ready to let go. Since your bastard of a husband spent your entire adult life convincing you how worthless you are, I guess we can't expect your mind to let go of that notion overnight, can we?"

She shook her head as she mulled on his words. "You could be right."

He picked up his spoon and dipped it into his soup. "Let's eat, kitten, before it gets cold."

She nodded, dipped her spoon, and took a careful sip from the lobster bisque.

Creamy liquid, the mild and slightly sweet taste of lobster, cognac, and a hint of cayenne burst on her tongue, and her eyelids dropped, and she moaned.

"That good, huh?" he teased.

When she opened her eyes, she met his now midnight blue stare, and her cheeks heated.

"It is," she said with all the dignity she could muster. "Why? Isn't your soup to your liking?"

"Oh, yes. I like it very much indeed." His eyes darkened further, and his cheekbones stood out more prominently.

She wasn't sure he was talking about soup anymore.

Before she could decide if she wanted to eat or talk, a shadow fell over her, and an unwelcome voice whispered, "Well, well, if it isn't the whore and her fuck of the month."

Michael Connolly stood closer than polite society allowed and—worse—too close for her comfort.

She shrank back in her seat.

"Leave my woman alone, Connolly." Byron's voice was colder than when he'd ripped the general management from the plant in Seattle a new one after the security audit.

"Your woman?" Connolly sneered. "The cunt is married to my friend."

"If you don't have something pleasant to say to

my companion, you might want to shut up altogether." Byron slowly rose. "Whatever you do, you will step back and keep a respectful distance, or I'll have you thrown out."

Connolly puffed out his chest. "You don't have the guts or the influence to do so."

"Don't I?"

There was so much silken menace in Byron's voice, Charlotte would have hidden under the table if it was directed at her. The whispering around them grew louder, and her breathing grew ragged. They were gathering an audience. Her heartbeat quickened and she felt sick to her stomach. Gasping, she clutched the edge of the table, trying to anchor herself.

Pushing Connolly aside, Byron was at her side in two swift steps. "Breathe through pursed lips and try to slow down."

"I can't," she gasped. "Not enough air."

"You have plenty of air, kitten. Slow down and breathe with me." He rubbed her back and ignored Connolly, who was smirking and making snide remarks.

"Sir, I must ask you to leave." An unfamiliar male voice said in an authoritative tone.

Oh no! Horror and mortification rose as a black-haired man in a designer suit with a displeased expression on his face halted at their table.

Is he kicking us out? Is he mad at us?

"Kittycat, concentrate on your breathing."

Connolly sputtered something she couldn't make out.

"You're disrupting the evening, and I need you to leave my restaurant."

His restaurant? Her eyes widened.

"You're kicking me out, what about them?" Spittle flew from Connolly's mouth and his eyes flashed.

"Honestly?" The manager gave Byron an exasperated eye-roll and resumed glaring at Connolly. "You think I'm going to kick the co-owner out?"

What?

Stunned into silence, her mouth dropped open as the manager and a muscled waiter dragged Michael Connolly away.

She swallowed and blinked. "You own this place?"

"I have a minor share."

"He has a bit more than a minor share."

Her head swiveled to the manager as he returned to their table. His almost black eyes sparkled with amusement and without the angry glare he was a good-looking man, she noticed.

"That man next to you is the sole reason Gusto Wine and Dine exists at all."

Her head swiveled back to Byron. Although he didn't look away from her face, he answered the man, "Nonsense, Sandro. Your business skills and talent, not to forget your nose, is responsible for the insane success of this establishment."

"Nose?" Her voice rose.

"Hmhm. Sandro here is the best wine connoisseur in the country." Byron's eyes softened. "And he's one of my closest friends."

"Oh?" Again, her gaze slid to Sandro. What a strange name. Somehow, she had the impression the title of best friend pleased Sandro more than the praise of his wine skills. Charlotte took an instant liking to the man.

He gave her an apologetic smile. "I'm sorry about the unpleasantness, miss."

She managed to wave her hand dismissively. "You have nothing to be sorry about. Thank you for escorting him out."

"My pleasure." He gave her a tight smile. "Forgive me for forgetting my manners." He gave her a slight bow. "Alessandro Lamberto, at your service."

Although her knees still shook, she softened her lips into a semblance of a smile and inclined her head. "Pleasure to meet you. I'm Charlotte."

Gradually, Charlotte relaxed and even engaged in a bit of small talk with Mr. Lamberto, who insisted she call him Sandro until their host needed to excuse himself. She gave Byron a brave smile. "Let's finish our starters before the soup goes entirely cold."

$$* * *$$

After their waiter served them coffee, Byron lifted her hand to his mouth and kissed her knuckles. She had been quieter than usual during the rest of their meal, clearly shaken by the encounter. He could kick himself for giving in to her wish to leave the penthouse. If he could, he would keep her there, where she was safe and shielded from the harsh outside world.

She blinked and gave him a brave smile. "Stop it."

He lowered his eyebrows. "What?"

"You are wondering how you can make this right. How you can protect me and shield me."

"Kitten."

She sat up straighter and stared him in the eyes. "No, don't. You can't shield me or keep me safe."

"What? Are you trying to depress me?" He tried to joke.

"I'm serious, Byron."

He stilled. She rarely used his name, and she'd never used it in this tone before.

"I realize you care for me and want to take care of me, and while that's fine and I appreciate it, I'm also sure I need to become strong in my own right. I can't expect you to always be there to handle my issues for me." She patted his hand like he was an overeager student.

He almost grinned.

"If I want my life to change, I have to change myself. Not by leaning on you or cowering behind you."

Speechless! She rendered him speechless with her bravery. While he thought she was scared and upset, her logical mind had been working on plans for her future. Not able to tell her with words how he admired her, he could show her. Byron pulled her in for a deep, drugging kiss—completely oblivious of their surroundings.

DAY NINETEEN

Dressed in a t-shirt she borrowed from Byron's closet, skimpy panties, and nothing else, Charlotte padded on bare feet through the silent penthouse. Her Master had left their bed at five in the morning, pressed a kiss to her forehead, and ordered her to go back to sleep. Now it was half past nine, and she needed to sort out some business for herself.

Since Byron would be spending the day in Seattle hiring new management, she only needed to take care of herself. But first, she wanted to do some research.

Although last night's encounter with Michael Connolly had been horrifying and mortifying, she didn't regret going out for dinner, and it gave her some valuable insights. She entered the quiet office room and switched on the light.

With a little over a week left, one of them was the need to find a job as soon as possible.

I'm never going to be dependent on another person again.

Her mind wandered to the scarred man, who never ceased to amaze her with his singular focus, tender care, and commanding presence, but she forced her mind back to the task at hand.

Her stomach grumbled, but she ignored the signal. She could eat later; first Charlotte wanted to go online job-hunting.

* * *

Three hours later, she shivered in the air-conditioned draft, for the first time realizing she was covered in goosebumps. She slammed the laptop shut.

Tapping her fingers on the smooth surface, she made a mental inventory and pinched her lips. Three hours, and she'd found nothing suitable.

Of course, she could work as a waitress or in cleaning, and she would if needed, but it wasn't what she liked to do. Those weren't long-term jobs. Working alongside Byron gave her a taste for business, but for a position as a secretary, personal assistant, or even receptionist she needed a degree and training.

Letting out a frustrated sigh, Charlotte rose

from the buttery-soft leather chair and paced the study. Most interesting jobs either required a high school diploma or a GED as well as some formal education.

She reached the tall windows but was oblivious to the stunning city skyline view. Turning on her heels, she held her head low and paced back to the desk.

"Maybe I can take an online course to get my GED. I must research how long that would take." Not even realizing she spoke out loud, she almost bumped into the desk. Turning again, she folded her hands on her back.

"Okay, I'm not dumb, my grades were excellent when Liam convinced me I didn't need a degree for marriage." Reaching the window, she pivoted and paced back.

But how am I going to pay for food and shelter, let alone schooling?

Ignoring her shivers, she plopped down on the luxurious office chair, sending the seat spinning. Whoa! Lightheaded, she gripped the edge of the desk and realized she should get something to eat. But the internet called to her, and she unfolded the laptop to open again. The screen sprang to life, and Charlotte started typing.

* * *

Her head swimming with fatigue and dizziness, she barely registered when the elevator dinged, and the door slid open revealing an exhausted Byron. Holding his jacket by his index finger over his shoulder, his shirt was rumpled, and the scars on his face were pronounced, like lines carved into a marble statue.

His lips pressed together as he took her in. "Are you still in your sleepwear?"

She shot up from the chair and put out her hand to steady herself on the desk. Oh no, she was dizzy and tired. Blinking, she tried to remember his question. Oh, her clothes. She looked down at her body as if to remind herself what she was wearing and blinked again. "Oh, um, yes. I. You. I." Not knowing what to say, she stumbled to a halt and stared at her feet.

If only I wasn't so lightheaded.

"What have you done today? Didn't you take care of yourself at all, kitten?" His tone wasn't stern, but there was a hint of censure in it, and she bristled.

Okay, so yes, I haven't taken much care of myself today, but figuring out my future is important to me. But maybe not to him. Because he wants to keep me? Control me?

Another wave of vertigo assaulted her, and her stomach revolted.

"Sorry, Sir. It all took longer than I realized."

He took a step into the study, his head tilted, and his eyes trained on her face. "All what?"

But she couldn't answer. Her stomach did another cartwheel, and bile rose in her throat. Oh, my Goodness! Her eyes wide, she slapped a hand over her mouth.

I'm going to throw up.

"I'm sorry" she muttered again before rushing past him. Hurrying through the hallway, she cursed the size of the penthouse. She stumbled through the bedroom and into the bathroom before dropping on her knees in front of the toilet bowl with an agonized grunt.

Clutching the cold porcelain, she heaved painfully, her empty stomach clenching and protesting.

Behind her heavy footsteps fell to the tiled floor as Byron entered the bathroom. Her face wet with tears and sweat, she tried to say something, but another round of violent heaves stole her breath.

A comforting hand massaged her nape, as her body shuddered and struggled through the nausea.

Still embracing the porcelain and exhausted, Charlotte sank to one hip and tried to convince her body there wasn't anything to expel.

A glass appeared in front of her, and she accepted the water with shaking hands.

"Better?" Byron wet a washcloth to wipe her face and took the glass from her. After rinsing out the cloth, he placed his palm with the damp fabric on the back of her neck.

She took stock of her body. The water helped, and so did the cool washcloth as well as his support. "A little."

"Are you ready to leave the floor?"

"Uhuh." Unsure if she meant it as a confirmation or denial, Charlotte let go of the toilet bowl.

The sound of the toilet flushing made her cheeks heat, and then he carefully lifted her and carried her to the bed.

"Hang on a moment, kitten."

She watched as his long legs carried him out of the bedroom before she curled on her side.

What on earth made me this sick?

Byron didn't give her much time to worry about the question because he returned with a food tray.

"I can't eat now." She struggled into a sitting position.

"Have you eaten at all today?" He handed her a cup with warm liquid. "Take a small sip and see how your stomach handles it."

Reluctantly, she accepted the mug and took a tentative sip. Her throat and esophagus burned, and she almost handed the tea back but dutifully took another drink. This time the fluid went down more smoothly. Something must have shown in her face because he rumbled his approval and sank down on the bed.

A little more alert now, she stretched her neck and peeked at the tray.

He must have followed her gaze. "Do you want to try a saltine cracker?"

She nodded.

* * *

Byron stroked Charlotte's calf and kept a close eye on her. A little color returned to her face, and she wasn't shivering anymore, but she still worried him. Why hadn't she taken better care of herself today? Should he have checked? Too many questions, and too few answers.

Charlotte finished her cracker and gave him a watery smile. "Thank you."

Forcing himself to tip up the corners of his mouth, he cocked his head. "How are you feeling?"

"Better now."

Taking a deep breath, he tried to control his emotions. She seemed to notice his concern because she placed her palm over his stroking hand and squeezed once. "Really, I am feeling much better. It's just I got preoccupied with research and forgot to eat. That's all."

That's all? Unreal!

He pinched the bridge of his nose with his free hand. "Let's address your apparent incapability to take care of your own body later because, quite frankly, I am displeased with the way I found you tonight. But you also made me curious. What was so interesting or important on the internet?"

"Will you sit with me, while I tell you?" She patted the mattress on her other side, and he gave her his first real smile for the evening.

"Of course, I will." After toeing off his shoes, he rounded the bed, settled next to her, and pulled her in.

She snuggled into his side and let out a contented sigh. Then she started to tell him about jobs and requirements, GEDs and other studies.

Again, she blew him away with her intelligence, endurance, and her courage. That didn't mean he was pleased with some of her decisions today, but he had nothing to say other than that she was fucking awesome.

2 0

DAY TWENTY

Entering the dining room the following morning, she halted in her tracks and stared at the flat box with a golden bow. Per his request, she'd prepared two plates.

"Ah, good morning, Kittycat. Right on time with breakfast. Very good." He shook out his napkin and placed it on his lap. An irrational twinge of envy shot through her as the linen settled on his thighs.

That's my place.

Sliding her gaze from the man waiting to the package and back, she made her way into the room. In the light of the new morning, yesterday's events embarrassed Charlotte even more. Events she could have prevented had she listened to her body instead of pressing on with her online research. A mistake she made once too often for her own liking.

She placed his plate in front of him and stole a

glance at his face—although he was well-versed in schooling his features when in business or at the poker table, his expressions when in her presence were easier to read. Now, however, he kept his facial muscles in a friendly and relaxed expression, but she didn't miss the shadows in his eyes as if his inner sun was clouded. She swallowed and hurried to the other side of the table. "I'm sorry about last night."

He waited for her to place her own breakfast and take the seat opposite of him before he reacted, "What is it you're sorry about?"

Charlotte bowed her head. "I'm ashamed for forgetting to take care of me." She lifted her face and met his stare straight on. "What grown woman can't take care of her own basic needs?"

"Ah, kitten." He tilted his head and toyed with his fork. "You would be surprised how many, but that isn't the point. Since a very young age, you have been the caregiver—which is as ingrained in your personality as its trait is nurtured in you. First, by taking care of your grandfather. Later, by trying to appease an impossible-to-please asshole of a husband." Some of the fire returned in his eyes. "For the last couple of weeks, I made sure you took care of yourself as much as you tend to my needs and wants. I want to apologize, too."

Her head jerked back. "You do? Why?"

Holding out his hand, he pinned her with his

stare. She dropped her hand in his palm, and he immediately closed his fingers around hers. "I should have made some arrangements for you. Left you a schedule, clothing, something to anchor you."

"But I shouldn't need an anchor."

His fingers squeezed hers. "Baby, everybody needs an anchor, even the strongest of us do."

"You don't."

"No?"

She pondered on the notion and came up with nothing. Byron patiently waited for her. She loved how he never made her feel stupid nor insignificant. Her thoughts and opinions were important to him. But he didn't need her or any other person to keep him stable and afloat. Or did he? She gave him a questioning look.

A slow smile crept from the corners of his mouth to his cheeks, and his eyes lightened. "Nothing?"

"Um, no. I don't think you need anybody."

"You're mistaken. Having you here. Taking care of you and protecting you—even from yourself—and seeing you bloom and grow settles something inside me. Your need to be guided and dominated is as large as my need to control you and help you thrive. There's nothing more effective than to have your soft body on my lap or yielding beneath me to settle my anger or frustration, like with the Seattle safety issues. And there's nothing more to say I'm loved and trusted than when you willingly submit to my"—his mouth curved—"baser needs, and to implements of pain and pleasure."

"Oh." The word left her mouth on a soft sigh.

"Do you want to eat first, or unwrap your present?" He indicated the wrapped gift with his head.

"For me? Why?"

"Do I need a reason to give you a present?"

Um yes. Gifts never came free. At least, with Liam they didn't—few and far between as they were.

"Huh, maybe you don't. I do seem to be conditioned to expect the worst though." She chewed on her bottom lip and leaned back in her chair. "Now I remember how Poppa used to bring me gifts. We didn't have much, but he always brought me something when he came home—an apple, a pretty rock, some candy." Her heart lifted with the memory. "He gave freely and with all his heart."

"That's it, Kittycat." He inclined his head, but even the shadows couldn't conceal his smile. "Now unwrap this one."

Charlotte's eyes widened when she opened the box, revealing the rose-gold MacBook and the latest model iPhone. With an awed expression, she stroked her fingertip over the laptop. "Are those for me?"

He chuckled and gave her a "what do you think" look.

Her gorgeous eyes brimmed with tears as she looked up at him and sucker-punched him right in the gut.

A long breath escaped her, and she closed the box as if it contained a bomb. "I can't accept. I won't."

"Why not?"

She let out a long-suffering sigh. "I'm not comfortable with accepting gifts. You've already given me an eReader and these are... are far more expensive. It makes me feel cheap."

"Kitten." Displeasure, disbelief, and hurt dripped from the one word, and Byron couldn't care less.

She stiffened but maintained eye contact.

Scooting back his chair, he slapped the napkin beside the rapidly cooling breakfast and patted his thigh. "Come here."

She bit her lip.

Her hesitation scraped his nerves like concrete once scraped his skin, but then she reluctantly rose and slowly moved around the table.

She perched on his knee like a small child would do with a distant relative, rather than cuddling close as he'd come to love. Fuck that! He wrapped his arms around her waist and yanked her against him —not delicately at all.

"Now tell me why you're objecting. I want you to have a phone. If you worry about the costs, don't. It comes with a year-long paid plan, including internet access. It's small enough to fit in a purse or a back pocket but has a six-and-a-half-inch screen, so you can use it for reading, too." She opened her mouth to reply, but he placed his index finger against her lips. It pleased him immensely when she obeyed his silent order, and some of his frustration drained away. His shoulder muscles unknotted.

"Now for the MacBook. When you're going to school, you'll need a laptop." He shrugged. "I figured you would rather get something useful than jewelry or designer clothes." Okay, he did buy her more of those, too, but that's beside the point now. Now, he needed her to accept the devices.

Charlotte pressed her back against his bicep and tipped back her head. "I agree I need a laptop for school, but it doesn't have to be something high-end like that." She worried her mouth and gestured to the box on the table.

He lifted the shoulder she wasn't leaning against. "Only the best is good enough for you, and I can afford the best the market has to offer."

"I know you can, but that isn't the point, is it? I don't want you to buy me expensive things. To me, it cheapens what's between us." She placed her soft palm against his marred skin with the tenderest of touches. "I love you for who you are, not what you can buy me."

He'd learned at an early age that life didn't give a damn about being fair. Hell, not only wasn't it fair, it could rise up and tear your world apart in the span of a single breath and then turn around and rip the very soul from your body. Whining about it was a colossal waste of time and energy. When one's world imploded, a person had two choices: give up or fight like hell.

He'd chosen the latter, working hard his entire life to get where he was to gain the knowledge and experience necessary to run not one but several businesses that employed thousands of people. Though he liked to believe those same people respected him, he was savvy enough to acknowledge they were far more likely to simply appreciate the fact that he signed their paychecks. That had always been enough for him before.

The circles he walked in were filled with some of the wealthiest and most powerful people in the state. Years of experience and observation had proven that people often hid behind masks; one moment extolling your accomplishments and the next attempting to stomp you into the ground. One didn't reach the pinnacle of success without learning how to look behind the façade, and he'd long since stopped basing his own worth on the accolades of others.

But now, hearing Charlotte state that she loved him for who he was... and not give a damn about what his money could give her, made him feel emotions he'd never experienced before. He'd won awards aplenty and yet not a single one had made him feel as honored as the woman sitting on his lap did every single day. Looking down into eyes that never failed to make his heart beat just a little faster, he smiled.

"I know that, Kittycat, and I love you as well." Her eyes softened and yet the firm set of her lips told him she needed more. Lifting his hand, he stroked a fingertip across slightly downturned lips before cupping her face in his palm. Bending forward, he brushed her mouth with his own, the very taste of her enough to make his cock twitch. By the time he pulled back, her face was flushed with desire and far more than her eyes had softened. Her entire body was pliable against his.

"May I ask you a favor?"

"A favor?" she parroted as if the very concept was foreign to her.

He had to force himself not to reveal how the shock in her expression and in her tone made him want to smash his fist into Randall's face. It was painfully obvious the bastard had never once considered asking rather than demanding anything of his wife, much less acknowledging the fact that being in Charlotte's presence was a gift greater than any business deal could ever offer.

A soft hand came up to cover his own, bringing him back to what mattered. "I didn't mean to upset you, Sir. I was just surprised... I mean you don't have to... the very fact you asked..." She paused and shook her head. "What I'm trying to say, and doing a very poor job of it, is that, yes, of course you may."

He slipped his hand from beneath hers, capturing it and placing a kiss upon her palm. "Allow me this, Kittycat. You may not need or even want it, but I promise it has absolutely nothing to do with money. Being able to pamper you brings me great pleasure. I know it's hard for you, that I'm asking a lot, but, please, allow me to spoil you."

She stiffened slightly, the battle going on in her head obvious as her expression shifted and yet he was already beginning to smile when she finally nodded.

"Thank you," he said, bending down to kiss her much more forcefully this time. Pulling back, he wrapped his arms tighter around her, shifting her body as he started to stand.

"Oh!" she gasped as he adjusted her so that she was facing him. Her legs lifted to wrap around his waist as his arms dropped to provide a shelf for her ass to rest on. "Wait! What about the food?" she said as he walked away from the table.

"I've decided I'd rather have you for breakfast," he growled. Her giggle turned into a moan when he leaned down to nip at the sweet spot where her shoulder met her neck.

It was lunchtime before they reappeared and as he watched Charlotte move about the kitchen wearing nothing but his t-shirt, knowing she was completely bare beneath the fabric, he reassessed his earlier thought. Yes, while life would never be fair, would always be messy and filled with challenges as well as grief, it was one hell of a ride and fabulous beyond words when you had someone to share it with.

DAY TWENTY-ONE

"Randall." Byron squeezed the bridge of his nose and tried to rein in his temper.

"Nolan." Charlotte's soon-to-be ex-husband answered with the same lack of warmth in his voice.

Byron glanced over to his kitten, whose shoulders had stiffened at her husband's name. Striving for a neutral tone, he said into the phone "Why are you calling me?" Despite his efforts, his voice wasn't the least bit welcoming.

He'd come to loathe the other man, and every detail Charlotte revealed about her life with the bastard made his hatred grow. He wasn't in the mood for polite conversation, but face it, Liam was still her husband and his business associate, so as much as he wanted to simply ignore the call, he knew he had to take it.

However, Byron didn't see any reason to draw it out. "State your business, Randall."

"Now, now"—the other man's chuckle grated like fingernails on a chalkboard—"is that a way to greet your business partner and the husband of your temporary fuck toy?"

He had no idea if Randall was taunting him with the temporary remark or hoped Charlotte would overhear his derogatory address. He'd wager it was actually a bit of both since he hadn't seemed too pleased at seeing them together at the charity event.

If he wasn't involved in any of the man's businesses, he would have ruined him financially by now. Then again... He squinted into the distance and his attention went inwards. He could afford losing money on Randall's real-estate business, but the bastard couldn't. It might be worth the few million bucks just to rid himself and Charlotte of the asshole.

Meanwhile, Randall was blabbering into his ear, and while he didn't particularly care, he wanted the call to be over with quickly and forced himself to listen.

The guy rambled a bit about business, and Byron leaned back in his chair and watched Charlotte. She'd resumed her work, and he admired her graceful efficiency. Her movements had become more secure over the last couple of days, and she'd settled in his company. She trusted him and seemed to enjoy the work. In no way was he going to allow her to return to the bastard and be forced into the meek housewife role again.

As if conjured by his thoughts, Randall's next words snapped Byron's attention back to the phone call.

"I was wondering if you could part from your fuck toy two days earlier?"

Byron shot upright at the man's words. "Two days earlier? Why?"

Charlotte turned around with an alarmed expression on her face, and he forced a smile and gave a swift shake of his head.

Her shoulders relaxed and she turned back to her task.

"I'm having a party on Sunday, and I need her to take care of the guests."

Byron clenched his hand around the phone. "Hire a fucking caterer." His words came out guttural.

Randall let out another nasty chuckle. "Ah, well. Sure, a caterer could take care of some of the needs my guests have, but not all."

Byron closed his eyes in disgust and pinched the bridge of his nose. Charlotte was not going back to this bastard—not in his lifetime. Not even if he had to keep her prisoner in his penthouse for the rest of her life.

Realizing he had to be very careful with his

response for both Charlotte and Randall, he curtly reminded, "That wasn't the deal."

"I can compensate you."

"How?"

"Name your price."

"This... asset is priceless."

"Come on, it's not like her pussy is made of gold or something. I find her rather dull and unresponsive unless she's screaming with pain. She has a nice scream. Sadly, she doesn't scream easily. Not even Connolly can get her to scream much anymore."

Byron ground his back teeth so forcefully, they might have cracked. He wouldn't extend a hand to the man if he were drowning, and the Devil would be ice-skating in hell before he'd give up Charlotte. "A deal is a deal, Randall."

"Fuck man, can't you give a friend a break?"

"You're not my friend, and you're the one who made the deal, remember?"

"I know that," Randall whined. "Fuck, man, I can give you the money now."

This time it was Byron's turn to give a mirthless chuckle. "No, you can't. I'm going to hold you to the deal, and that's final."

Byron pulled the phone from his ear and pushed the disconnect button on the screen, cutting off the sound of Randall's protest. He exhaled through his nose and fought back the urge to throw his phone across the room. Ending a call with an old-fashioned landline would at least have given him the satisfaction of slamming the receiver down.

A welcome presence at his side distracted him, and he slid the cellphone into his pocket. "Kittycat." He shuffled back to create room for her and pulled her on his lap.

She curled her arms around his neck and cuddled against him.

He inhaled her light floral scent and tightened his arms around her. "What can I do for you?"

She pushed herself up with her hands on his shoulders and tipped her head back. "Funny, that was what I wanted to ask you."

He pressed a kiss to her nose and gathered his thoughts. Testing the water, he volunteered, "That was Liam calling."

She didn't show any emotion in her face but her hands on his shoulders tightened to the point of discomfort. "I guessed as much."

"We're three weeks into our agreement, and I want to discuss how to continue after this. What are your plans?"

She swallowed and worried her lip. He stroked the pad of his thumb over her mouth and freed the flesh from between her teeth. If her mouth was swollen it would be from his kisses. Byron hated to unsettle her, but they needed to talk and sooner rather than later.

She opened and closed her mouth, stared over

his shoulder at a point on the wall, and heaved a sigh.

Curling his hand around her cheek, he returned her gaze to his face. "Charlotte, I love you. I would like for you to stay with me."

Her entire body stiffened, and tears pooled in her eyes. "There's nothing I would rather do, but I don't think I should."

* * *

His face darkened, and his scars became more pronounced. His shoulder muscles under her hands bunched with tension, and he radiated unhappiness.

She stroked the sides of his neck with her index fingers and kept her hands on his shoulders. Her mind raced, as she tried to find the courage to talk about her plans.

"Hey"—he curled his hand around her cheek —"tell me, baby. Whatever it is that's on your mind, you can tell me."

"I know." And she really did. His consistency, his patience, his... well, his everything told her of his sincerity. It would be so easy just to accept his offer to remain, but she knew that while it would be the far easier path, it wasn't the one she was meant to take. She blinked hard and took a fortifying breath.

"I would love to stay with you, but I don't think that would be the right decision." She swallowed and fought back the tears threatening to spill over. "Part of the reason I stayed with Liam is that I'm dependent on him. If I would stay with you, I would interchange the man I'm relying on." She pressed her fingers against his mouth, determined to get him to understand. "I don't fear you'll ever take advantage of my dependence. I don't!" She implored him with her gaze "But I want to be able to rely on myself for a change. I need to know I can do it myself. Does that make any sense at all?"

"Yes." His voice sounded muffled against her hand. She chuckled despite her inner turmoil and tried to pull her hand away. He circled her wrist, held her hand in place, and kissed her fingertips before he lowered her hand to their laps and nodded. "I don't like to be mentioned in the same sentence with the bastard, but I understand how you feel. At least, I think I do. So, what are you planning to do, kitten?"

She chewed her lip and released it when his gaze dropped to her mouth. "I have a few ideas running through my head. Getting a job, going back to school." She lifted one shoulder. "I'm not sure, yet. As soon as I make up my mind, I would like to run it past you."

"That sounds fine to me, and you still have time," Byron acquiesced. He swallowed. "And what about your husband?"

A shudder ran through her as she sat up a bit

straighter. "I won't go back to him. Even if I have to sleep under a bridge and have to stand in the bread-line for the rest of my life."

Master gripped her face between both of his hands. "That will never happen—not over my dead body." He crashed their mouths together in a vora-cious kiss, ending their conversation in an exceed-ingly pleasant way.

22
DAY TWENTY-TWO

"How are you doing today?" Byron grabbed Charlotte's wrist as she placed the stack of printed and bundled contracts on his desk. Organized and intelligent, she did most of the preparations these days, and he had yet to find a mistake in her work.

Although she stiffened for a moment, she allowed Byron to guide her around the desk and between his legs. She picked at the cuticle of her right thumb, and he took both her hands in his.

"I should—" She turned her gaze to the filing cabinet, but he tugged on her hands and redirected her attention back to him.

"Answer my question."

Concentrating on keeping his face impassive, he studied the barrage of emotions flooding over her face and silently waited.

Her shoulders heaved as she expelled air from her lungs. "I guess I was rattled more than I'd thought by Liam's call yesterday, but I'm fine now." His expression must have conveyed his annoyance as she added, "No really, I'm fi... I'm good, um, okay. Whatever."

Her pout was cute, and he wanted to lean forward and kiss her. But talking was more important now than lust or even love. He hummed and waited.

She threw him a scowl. "I haven't figured out how I'm going to do everything when the month is over, but I'm pleased with my decision to go my own way."

He stiffened.

"I am aware you don't like it," she said before pulling one hand from his grasp and stroking his cheek. "But can't you see I need to do this? For myself?"

He did. "Yes, kitten, and as I told you yesterday, I understand why you would want it. True, I don't like it. I love you, baby, and I want to take care of you. That's going to be hard for me to do if you're not around."

Charlotte pursed her lips. "That's true. But you gave me a phone. It's not like we can't talk or—or meet. It's just..." She trailed off.

He finished for her. "You want to be sure you can stand on your two own feet as an independent woman before you commit to another relationship."

"Yes. Also, technically, I'm still married to Liam. I don't want to give his lawyers—you realize he will lawyer up, right—any leverage by claiming I'm an unfaithful slut or something like that."

Okay, he didn't like the sound of that.

She softly laughed. "You can stop grinding your teeth. It's not how I view myself, but Liam will fight, and I'm pretty sure he will fight dirty."

There was no question that she would be right about that.

He interlaced their fingers. "I agree he will. I don't think living with me would make a difference, though. He's too scared of me and what I can do to his business. I can protect you, Kittycat."

Her eyes softened. "I know you can."

He sighed and decided to let the topic go. After all, he still had a week left to convince her otherwise. If all else failed and she left, he'd make damn sure she would experience freedom and independence, and it would be a positive experience. "All right," he replied. "I will let it rest for now. But I expect you to tell me if you change your mind. Okay?"

She nodded. He cupped her cheeks and pressed a kiss to her forehead.

"Now, tell me." He narrowed his eyes. "Did Liam's call bring back any ugly memories?"

* * *

Why can't he just leave things well enough alone?

Frustrated, Charlotte leaned away from him but when she tried to tug away her hands, his grip tightened. "Why do you always have to dig into things? Into me?" She tugged again, and he let out a rumbling warning.

"Talk to me."

Charlotte let out a derisive snort and pitched her voice low. "Talk to me, baby." In her own voice, she added, "Just stop with the domineering act. I might like it in the bedroom, but I don't want to be bossed around here."

One eyebrow slid up.

"And don't use that look on me."

"What look?"

"The 'Daddy isn't mad, Daddy is disappointed' one."

"I'm not your daddy."

"No, you're not. But you are being an asshole, who is constantly probing me to bare my soul and who won't be honest about his own past with me."

Finally, he let go of her hands, and she took a hasty step back and folded her arms.

He sighed and eyed her warily. "What do you want to know?"

"What happened to your leg?"

"Busted kneecap."

Um, okay, well that didn't tell me much, does it?

"How did you bust it?"

"Bad luck."

She sniffed and tried again. "Bad luck how?"

"I was in a car crash."

His shoulders went stiff, and his entire body screamed his discomfort with the topic.

"What happened?"

He shrugged. "Just an accident."

The lines on his face and the shadows in his eyes told Charlotte there was a lot more to tell than that.

"You know, for a guy who relentlessly pressures me to open up and to be honest, you are being annoyingly evasive." She pushed out her bottom lip in a childish pout. "I don't like it."

He didn't laugh like she hoped he would. If anything, he closed off even more.

Suddenly cold and oddly disappointed, she curled her arms around her upper body in a self-hug and stroked up and down her arms. "Whatever."

Her attempt of stomping out of the room was hampered by a long, muscled arm around her waist. Byron rested his head against her belly and whispered, "I'm sorry."

She lowered her face and pressed her cheek against the top of his head. As she stood in his arms and gave him comfort, she stroked his nape and shoulders. Whatever had happened had to be far more than "just an accident". All she could do was

let him know that she was there for him. As fingertips moved softly over his tense muscles until they
finally began to loosen, all she could hope was that
he'd decide he could confide in her and open up
about his past. The shadows changed as the sun
lowered, and Charlotte waited.

23

DAY TWENTY-THREE

Surprised, Charlotte followed Byron as he all but pulled her through the penthouse. "What? What's going on?"

"You'll see, kitten." His smile was wide and infectious, and he looked almost boyish and charming.

"Slow down." She chuckled and tried to keep up with his long stride.

He shortened his steps. "Sorry."

"No problem. I'm curious, though," she said as Byron guided her at a more moderate pace through the hallway. "What has you this excited?" They'd made love last night, and she slept in his arms all night. He might not have opened up to her about his past, but he had shown her with his body what he couldn't with his words.

Byron led her onto a secluded balcony, and she gasped.

"I figured you hadn't been here before, have you?"

Such a smug expression, but oh… he had all the reasons to be smug about this.

She double blinked. She'd seen Jacuzzis, but only at spas and saunas not in people's houses—on their balconies. Tipping her head back, she gazed up at her Master. As much as she liked his surprise, she loved seeing the sparkle in his eyes even more.

"You know," she teased, "it's good I wasn't aware of this sooner, or I wouldn't have had time to help you in the office." She enjoyed everything water, and a hot tub ranked high on her wish list—not that she ever talked with Liam about getting one. Her gaze returned to the Jacuzzi.

"Go on." He nudged her shoulder. "You can go in."

A bit uncertain, she gazed around and studied the glass partition.

"Don't worry. Not only do I own the entire building, but no one is here at this time of day, except for one security guard downstairs. No one can see through the privacy glass."

She almost bounced on her feet. "I would love to try."

Byron leaned down and took her mouth in a voracious kiss. Sooner than she wanted, he broke off and patted her butt. "Strip and hop in." He sauntered to the other side of the balcony and returned with a bottle of red wine and two glasses.

"Are you coming in with me?"

Pulling her flush against him, he whispered into her hair. "I would love to join you. Let me get towels and our bathrobes."

Giggling, she stripped to her birthday suit with a boldness she didn't realize she possessed until she met this amazing man.

When Byron returned shortly after, he made quick work of his clothing and hopped into the hot tub with her, splashing water in her face.

She giggled again.

"Whoops, sorry."

Stroking the drops from her face, she shook her head. "I won't melt from a little water."

He pulled her against his side and pressed a few buttons, engaging the jets.

Charlotte groaned in delight as the forceful stream frothed the surface of the water and burrowed closer to him.

"Now relax here for a while. You have been hunkered over your laptop for quite some time today. Any luck in finding decent jobs?"

He was so sweet and considerate. All he seemed to want to do was to take care of her. Always concerned about her comfort and well-being. It was nothing like she'd expected when she turned up here a little over three weeks ago.

She tipped her head back and stared up at him. "No, not really. I suppose I have to settle for a minimum-wage job or somehow make my way through school and get certified."

He hummed and played with the tendrils of hair at the nape of her neck.

That was something else she loved about him. He reserved judgment and gave a person time to think and explain themselves. Maybe because he was a private person himself. She narrowed her eyes on him. "You always ask questions about me, my day, and my plans, but you're tight-lipped about yourself and what happened in your past."

He stiffened.

"I don't ask, let alone demand, total openness from you. But I hope you know, I can keep a secret, and there won't be much I won't be able to accept." She tried to lighten the mood. "Since I've prepared your breakfast for a while now, I'm pretty certain you aren't some kind of Blackbeard who eats babies for breakfast. So, whenever you're ready, feel free to hit me with it. I promise I can handle whatever it is that's been eating you up for such a long time."

* * *

With his heart pounding in his throat, Byron regarded the little submissive in his care. Despite her little speech, she didn't demand, didn't even push him. She simply kissed his cheek before snuggling just a little bit closer. She was right but… opening up about his ugly past? He shuddered and inhaled through his nose. With Charlotte this close to him, her delicious scent mingled with the chlorine blended in the water. The jets hammering against sore muscles drowned out the pulsing of the blood through his veins.

He sighed, raked his hand through his hair, and tried to settle more comfortably. "When I was eighteen, I was in a car accident."

He stole a glance at her. Her expressive face usually showed her every emotion but in the dim light and through the haze the steam created, he found it hard to read her.

"It was the end of November, and we had some snow and sleet. My—" His voice broke, and he swallowed.

A small hand entangled with his beneath the surface of the bubbling water. She squeezed and rubbed their shoulders together.

"I lost my entire family that day: father, mother, and my younger brother. Garrett was thirteen when… he died. They all died." His eyes burned—damn chlorine.

He wanted to run from the tub, but swift as a monkey she straddled his lap and snuggled her face in the crook of his neck.

"Thank you for telling me this. It must have been

so hard to lose your family. You don't have to tell me anything more today. Now, just relax and enjoy the water."

Automatically, his arms went around her waist and he pulled her flush against him. Breathing her in, his muscles slowly unknotted, his racing heart slowed to a moderate pace, and his fraying emotions gradually settled.

They sat like that long enough for their skin to turn pruney and for the automatic balcony lights to switch on.

When she pushed again his chest, Byron opened his arms reluctantly. She tipped back her head, and he swooped in to take her offered lips—soft and warm, and ever so inviting. He reversed their positions and kissed down her body to suckle on her nipples. She arched into his ministrations, and he swooped her up into his arms. Ignoring the towels and bathrobes, he carried her inside the penthouse and lowered her onto a nearby couch. Goosebumps erupted on her skin.

"Cold?"

"Nu-huh." She shook her head. "I'm hot. I burn for you. Would you"—she peeked at him through long, dark lashes—"please make love to me, Sir?"

"Oh, I will. But first I'm going to make you come." He slid down her torso and went to do what he promised. Using his mouth, tongue, and fingers he gave her a massive orgasm in record time.

While she was still panting from the climax, he rose and admired the carnal visual. She was naked, flushed from the orgasm, and her breasts heaved with her rapid breathing.

Byron gripped the back of the couch with one hand and hooked the other at the crook of her knee. Spreading her open more widely, he stared at the junction of her thighs, where the pink flesh accepted all of him.

The wet slapping sounds echoed in the large living room and edged him on. He bucked his hips harder, pounding into her with abandon now. Watching her come had stoked his libido and he was determined to pour every last bit of cum he had into her. Sweat trickled down his back and his balls drew up. Not yet! He gritted his teeth and willed the climax back down.

With effort, he released his hold on the couch and licked the pad of his thumb.

She moaned, clearly understanding his intention. "Not again."

Amused, he placed the wet digit at the top of her mound, just above the clit. She had one more orgasm in her, and this time she would take him with her.

The muscles around his intruding shaft tightened and rippled, adding to his own pleasure. She screamed, and he slammed deep—one, two, three times. He stilled as he exploded inside her in jet after jet as her pussy milked him dry.

DAY TWENTY-FOUR

Rising from the couch, Byron clicked off the movie credits. Charlotte hurried to collect their glasses and the cheese plate. Although yesterday's talk helped, Byron felt stiff and even uncertain, and—although sweet and compliant—his kitten had been fairly wrapped up in her own mind the entire day. He watched her walk toward the kitchen. Time for another BDSM scene to enhance their connection and solidify their trust in each other.

* * *

Her Master had been quiet and withdrawn throughout the day. Not... cold exactly but she couldn't help but worry he regretted talking about the accident. Should she reassure him she wouldn't blab and break his confidence? Was she seeing

ghosts, reading too much into things? Bugger! Why
were man-woman interrelationships so difficult? If
she asked more about the event, would he view her
questions as prying into his private business?

"Kittycat."

She almost jumped out of her skin as his voice
halted her quizzing mind. "Yes, Sir?"

"I need a bit of time to set up for a scene. Please
go to my bedroom, strip, shave, use the Aloe Vera
cream from the counter, and then kneel on the
white rug in the Nadu position."

"Yes, Master." Swiftly, she wrapped the cheese
and placed the leftover food in the fridge before
hurrying to the bedroom.

Now, her mind went racing in an entirely
different direction. What was he planning? And
why the extra shaving and Aloe Vera? Wasn't that
ointment for sunburns?

She sure hoped his plan didn't include putting
her in a solarium. She was so not a fan of tanning.

With somewhat shaking hands, she untucked
her shirt from her skirt and whipped the stretchy
material over her head. Despite her nervous anticipation, or maybe because of it, her breasts were
already heavy and sensitive, and her nipples beaded
into tight points. As she slid her hands over her
body and into the waistband of her skirt, the trembling of her fingers increased. She longed to move
her hands to the apex of her thighs and stroke one

out. Instead, she dropped the skirt and her panties at once and stepped out of her pumps. The promise of the delayed gratification made her blood hum in her veins.

On the counter in the bathroom, she found the Aloe Vera, a pink disposable razor, and feminine shaving cream. His distinctive footfall in the adjacent bedroom spurred her into action.

* * *

Lighting the candle, the flame flickered in the draft from the bathroom and Byron resisted the urge to turn. He finished his preparations and mentally went over the scene he planned. Satisfied with his effort, he turned.

Kneeling with her knees spread wide, head down, and hands with the palms up resting on her knees, Charlotte was the epitome of a submissive woman and exuded femininity and seduction.

He ran his gaze over her creamy skin, and it amazed him what a difference a few weeks made. Now her blonde hair was full and gleaming and hanging freely around her shoulders, her skin was unblemished, and her curves were alluring. But not only had her physical appearance improved over the weeks, but her mental state and self-esteem had grown as well. The combination turned her into a beautiful, irresistible package.

"Look at me."

Without hesitation, she tipped back her head and their gazes collided. She was sexy and beautiful, and she realized it now.

Byron stepped aside to let her take in the prepared scene area. "What do you think tonight's scene will be?"

She cocked her head and a little crease appeared between her eyebrows. His lips twitched and he held back the smile.

"Um, if you were a mafioso, I'd say you're done with me." She fixed her gaze on the plastic sheet covering the bed.

The tension keeping his stomach knotted unleashed, and Byron threw back his head and roared. He hadn't laughed like this in a very long time. Talk about a vivid imagination!

When he quieted down and looked at his submissive, her eyes were still on him, and they danced with laughter. "It's good to know you have a creative mind, it makes scenes all the more fun." Still grinning, he motioned to the burning candle. "Any ideas about the candles?"

"Um, torch my dead body." She shook her head and turned serious. "I'm afraid wax play isn't making wax sculptures, is it?"

What? His eyebrows pulled up. "Um, no, it isn't."

Her gaze now landed on the fire extinguisher.

"And I suspect you haven't lit candles to create a romantic ambiance."

He grinned, offered a, "Nope," and patted the covered mattress. Charlotte pleased him greatly when she immediately rose and climbed on the bed. He bent to brush a kiss over her lips. "I appreciate your trust."

"Oh, I trust you all right." Nevertheless, she licked her lips and gave the burning candle a worried glance.

"Like with many BDSM play, wax play is about trust and letting go of the control. Hot wax can feel wonderful against your skin and can burn as well. It's up to the Dom what you'll receive."

She nodded. "But I have my safeword, right?"

"You will always have a safeword with me, kitten." He paused before he added, "In fact, I'm going to give you a choice today. Do you want me to bind you, or do you prefer to keep still yourself?"

She chewed her lip, and her eyebrows puckered in concentration. "I think it will be easier to keep still when bound, Sir."

"It certainly will." He dipped his head and studied her face. "Bindings it is."

After pulling the cuffs from under the mattress and buckling them around her wrists and ankles, he knelt beside the bed and leaned on his forearm beside her head. Her eyelids fluttered close, and her lips parted on a gentle sigh. She loved being in his bindings. He stroked a fingertip over the soft skin between her elbow and shoulder. "I love having you bound and open for me." He circled in a figure-eight pattern around her breasts. "I love how I can touch you, any way and anywhere I want to." He swooped down and took her mouth in a long hard kiss that had her panting and him longing for more. But they needed the connection from a little play first.

Byron pulled back and checked the candles. Earlier, he selected red, black, and white soy candles and looked forward to creating some art on the most beautiful canvas he'd ever laid his eyes upon.

After their time together, Byron knew Charlotte's pain tolerance, and although he'd used these candles before, he tried some on the inside of his wrist to make sure the temp would be bearable for her.

He noticed her stunning emerald orbs on him. "Ready?"

Her gaze didn't waver.

To compare her eyes with gemstones was wrong, though. Although emeralds were beautiful, they were also hard and cold, but her eyes were warm and gleamed with affection and love.

Yes, love!

"I can't believe the stuff I let you do." She dropped her head back on the pillow with a dramatic sigh. "I'm as ready as I'll ever be."

"If you don't like the wax, we'll stop, but I have a

notion you might enjoy this." Experimentally, he drizzled a red line on her upper leg, starting at her knee and moving to her hip.

Letting out a gasp, Charlotte stiffened and then relaxed.

"Well?"

"That's actually nice."

He pried the wax from her leg and inspected the spot. It pleased him that her skin had only slightly pinkened underneath. "Since certain parts of your body are more sensitive than others"—he lifted the candle high in the air above her breasts—"I'm going to ask you throughout the play about your comfort level. But now"—he gave her a devious grin—"we play."

* * *

Almost an hour later, Byron surveyed the streaks of red, black, and white against creamy skin. Charlotte was deep into subspace and still spread-eagled on the bed.

He himself was hyperaware of every moan and wiggle he elicited from her and was firmly in top space.

Where impact play could be a struggle for him between not doling out more pain than he was comfortable with and still giving enough to send his submissive flying, wax play always fulfilled both needs. That more than made up for the mess in his opinion.

The control it gave was one of the reasons wax play ranked high on his favorite activities list.

Depending on the submissive's needs, he could intensify the sensation by pouring the wax from near the skin or weaken the heat by giving the wax more time to cool by pouring it from farther away.

An added benefit for him was how applying layer upon layers of wax onto a human canvas created an attractive sight; plus, it was fun to do as well.

Byron unbuckled the cuffs and joined Charlotte on the bed. Drowsily, she snuggled into him, and he massaged her shoulders and arms.

After pressing a kiss to the top of her head, he whispered, "How are you feeling?"

A soft smile curved her lips. "Wonderful. Just… lovely." She stroked his chest in a soothing rhythm. "You?"

He hummed his satisfaction. "Great, too." How this abused woman could trust him and love him enough to submit never ceased to amaze him. His arm around her shoulder tightened. "You are an amazing woman, Kittycat. One of the bravest and strongest persons I've ever met. More than that, you make me braver and stronger as well."

She tipped back her head and stared up at him. "I do?"

Unable to resist, he kissed her upturned lips. "Hmhm, you do. How can I not trust you with my past, when you show me every single day complete openness and vulnerability?"

"Oh." She sighed, snuggled against his chest again, and confided, "I never considered it in such a way, but this makes sense to me."

They sat for a while without speaking.

"What do you think of the wax?"

"I didn't expect the hot wax to be so pleasurable"—she peered down her body—"or look so beautiful. Did you enjoy it?"

"What's not to enjoy?" He grinned. "Even better, we still have part of the scene left."

The crease between her eyebrows appeared. "We do?"

"Yup." He rolled her onto her back and took his old Amex Black Card from the nightstand. "Now you're going to experience the sensation of having the wax peeled off."

DAY TWENTY-FIVE

The following morning, Byron made love to his Kittycat as soon as she was awake. His movements slow and deliberate, his hands careful and gentle, and his mouth soft and tender, he stroked in and out of her. She was so warm and slick around him. When her inner muscles began to flutter around him, he licked the pad of his index finger and sought to bring her to pleasure before exploding inside her.

Still panting, he nuzzled her neck and warmth rushed through him as she curled her arms around his neck and pulled him against her. His crushing weight on top of her didn't seem to bother Charlotte in the least.

He indulged in a few moments of cuddling. Pressing up on his elbows, Byron kissed her cheek and enjoyed the feeling of warm, soft skin under his lips. Beneath his mouth he could feel her smile, and her bedroom eyes blinked up into his. "I love you, Byron Nolan."

He groaned. "I love you too, Kittycat mine." Swooping down, he took her kiss-swollen mouth as if their lives depended on it, pouring in every ounce of love and devotion he felt for her.

When he finally pulled back, they were both panting for air and her eyes gleamed tenderly with love and tears. "I love you, Byron, with all my heart. But—" her voice trailed off and she swallowed.

He rested his forehead on hers and finished her sentence, "But you're still married and not willing to jump headfirst into a new relationship."

Charlotte let out a shuddering breath and quietly replied, "Yes."

Sighing, he lifted his weight from her, rolled to his back, and stared up at the ceiling. "I understand. I wish things were different, but I do understand."

Maybe he didn't like that she was withholding her love from him, essentially was holding back from him, but… Byron sighed. He couldn't blame her for keeping pieces of herself shielded from him. Byron himself still hadn't told Charlotte all about the accident that changed his face and his life—his deepest shameful regret. He should get out of bed and shower, but he stayed put. No matter the amount of water and soap, he could never wash away his feelings of remorse and guilt. Never!

DAY TWENTY-SIX

The wax-play had smoothed away any remaining awkwardness between them, Charlotte thought as she worked alongside Byron on a takeover. The business was a struggling publisher and Charlotte couldn't understand the problem. "I thought the publishing business was doing well with the current situation and people staying home."

"Hmm?"

She grinned and waited for him to tear his gaze away from the papers before she addressed him again and confided, "I find the way you focus and concentrate really sexy, Sir."

His eyes flashed, and a sexy smirk curved his mouth. "Do you now?"

All his attention now centered on her, sending tingles over her entire body—shivers of the pleasurable kind she'd come to love and anticipate. The air between them shifted with sexual tension, transforming him from boss into Master and her from assistant into submissive.

Byron rolled his chair away from the desk, and she was moving toward him before he held his hand out.

Sitting on his lap, she toed off her shoes and, curling her leg around his, rubbed the instep of her bare foot against his calf. He rested his chin on her shoulder and blew out his breath.

She leaned her upper body against his chest and enjoyed his warmth. For a moment, she just inhaled his unique amber scent.

"So, Kittycat, what did you ask me?"

Ask him? As if she could remember anything with his scent and strength enveloping her and a distinctive bulge growing against her behind. She wiggled, and his arms tightened.

"Kitten."

Her mouth quirked at the dominant, admonishing tone. "Yes, Sir?" She tipped her head back and stared up at his face.

He bent forward, but instead of kissing her lips, he clamped his teeth around her chin, and his midnight blue eyes blazed into hers. He let go of his hold, but shifted his arm behind her back, forcing her to lean back and trust him to keep her suspended. "You're being a brat. Answer my question."

"Oh, right, I remember. I asked why the publisher was having troubles since eBooks are doing well right now."

"Ah." He rubbed their noses together. "You're right about that. But when a publisher loses its reputation amongst authors and they don't want to write for them anymore, they get into problems."

"How come?"

"Romance readers are ferocious bibliophiles. They want new books, maybe not daily but every week. If a publisher doesn't deliver, readers find books elsewhere."

"And they might never return to the publisher because they found books they like at other places."

"Yes."

He nuzzled her neck, and Charlotte giggled. Her hands rose, and she tried to push his head away.

Her Master lifted his head and gave her his sternest expression. "Hands behind your head."

She obeyed without hesitation and then pouted. "I love you and everything you do, but it's not fair of you to expect me to keep my wits together when you turn me on like this."

The corner of his mouth lifted. "I turn you on?"

She scoffed. "You know you do."

He blasted her with a megawatt smile, agreed, "Yes, I do," and buried his face in her neck.

At the carnal onslaught, she pressed her thighs together to alleviate some of the ache in her core. In all her married years, Liam never elicited so much as a sliver of lust, and Byron only had to move his lips from her shoulder to her ear and she was dripping wet and ready for sex.

A sharp nip at the pulse at the base of her neck made her gasp and squeal.

"No thinking of the bastard."

Unreal. "How on earth—"

"Did I follow where your mind went?" he finished for her. "I see you, Kittycat. You brace yourself when you think of him, and your face turns as lifeless as a mask."

"Oh… I think less and less of him to be honest."

"Good!"

Charlotte giggled again but soon sobered. "I should probably start searching for a cheap divorce lawyer."

Now, her Master tensed. "We will find an excellent lawyer for you and not a cheap one. In fact, let me call my attorney. Garrick might be a corporate lawyer, but he should know someone who can help." He reached for his phone.

Charlotte stilled his movement by placing her palm over his hand.

Tilting his head, he arched a brow in an obvious, "what?"

"I can't afford an expensive lawyer."

His eyes softened. "You don't need to, I can."

As exasperation, indignation, and a well of love

warred inside her for supremacy, Charlotte quietly asked, "Why should you pay for my divorce?"

Gripping her shoulders, he turned her, putting them face to face. "Compromise with me on this, please." He swallowed and loosened his grip. "I'm not going to stop you from leaving in a few days. I'm not going to force you to work for my company. I respect you and your decision to find your own way in life. I don't like it, but I understand your need. I'm a Dom, kitten, and I love you. It's going to be super hard not to interfere in your life, and I do want to figure out with you how you can accomplish your goals with me still being part of your life." He dropped his forehead to hers. "Please, don't shut me out completely."

The room was silent except for their breathing for several long moments.

"I won't, Sir."

His chest heaved. "Thank you."

"That still doesn't explain why you should hire a lawyer for me."

His lopsided grin melted her heart and she almost agreed right away, but Charlotte bit her tongue.

"Liam is going to fight hard and fight dirty. He might not love you but he's not a man to let go of his assets easily."

Charlotte scoffed. "I'm not an asset to him."

Byron cocked his head. "I think you are, but let's

keep that for another time. Liam has the money and the connections to make it hard for you to divorce him. You're going to have enough on your plate as it is. Please, let me handle this for you."

If his logic wouldn't have swayed her, his plea would have. Byron rarely used the word please, and it took the wind right out of her. She suddenly realized that being an independent woman and making it on her own didn't mean refusing help when it was offered. Charlotte slung her arms around his neck. "All right, Sir. I'll let you handle the lawyer stuff." Then she mashed their mouths together, showing him her gratitude and how much she adored him.

DAY TWENTY-SEVEN

After calling his trusted corporate lawyer and arranging a meeting with—according to Rick Garrick—the best divorce lawyer in Missouri, Byron set out to find his submissive. Checking his watch, he went to the indoor gym, expecting her to be doing her exercises. It turned out he didn't need to wait to reach the gym. By the time he entered the hallway, the thumping of fists, grunts, and pounding of feet reached his ears.

When he entered the open door to the exercise room, Byron halted and admired the sight.

Gone was the scared little mouse, and in its place was a little firecracker punching her fists and feet into a pounding bag like it had personally insulted her. Perfectly balanced on the ball of her left foot she rotated from her hip and slammed her right foot in the bag. If it would have been a person, the kick would have landed on the knee and without a doubt crippled them.

Good. A downed man can't hurt her.

Charlotte was glorious like this and completely focused, which explained her startled reaction, when she turned for her water. Byron reached the bottle first, bent at the waist, and handed the water and a towel to her.

"Thank you." She accepted the offerings with a gracious smile, took a large swig of the water, and draped the towel over her shoulders. "Did you need something, Sir?"

Byron stroked a lock of sweat-streaked hair from her face. "Come here." He took her hand and escorted her to the bank press. After sitting down on the bench, he pulled her on his lap.

"I'm filthy," she protested weakly but didn't struggle against his hold.

"Nonsense, there's nothing wrong with a little workout sweat," he stated and pressed his nose in her hair. "I came to tell you about my call with Rick Garrick, my lawyer."

He relayed the gist of his call with Rick and informed Charlotte about the meeting with the divorce lawyer.

Charlotte sighed. "Thank you. I know I was reluctant to let you arrange this lawyer business, but I was way out of my depth." In a seemingly unconscious manner, she ran the tip of her nose over his neck and halted at the hollow below his throat. "So, now we wait."

"Yes." He swallowed.

Charlotte tipped her head back. "What's the matter?"

Byron swallowed. "I—I want to tell you all about what happened to my family."

She stilled. "Okay."

Byron sighed and he thought back to the morning that changed his life irrevocably.

"Damn it, boy. You're late." His father's black eyebrows slashed in a displeased V.

"I know, sir. I'm sorry." Byron squinted against the low sun. The reflection from the iced-over world intensified his hangover.

Thomas Nolan, the stern father, hardworking handyman, and volunteer firefighter placed his hand on Byron's shoulder. "I get it, son. I understand you wanted to celebrate with your team, but you know Garrett…" His father's voice trailed off.

Yes, Byron knew his brother and how badly he handled deviations from the routine.

But damn it, we won the State championship and having to go on a trip with my family sucks.

He followed his father to the car and smothered a sigh. Last night, he had been looking forward to some fun times with Angel, but his on-again off-again girlfriend hadn't even come to the game to cheer him on. And didn't that just suck as much as having to wake up early after a night of partying and drinking?

"Come on, boy," his father urged him, "we might get stuck in a traffic jam, and there's a flight to catch. Your mother and brother are waiting in the car."

Hoisting his sports bag higher on his shoulder, Byron bristled at the "boy". He hadn't yet celebrated his nineteenth birthday but already stood at six feet, five inches. Ripped with muscles from training and religiously working out, he considered himself a man.

After stuffing his bag in the cramped luggage area—mostly suitcases with stuff for his mother and Garrett—he plonked down on the backseat behind his mother and wished her and Garrett good morning. It earned him no reaction whatsoever from his brother and only a stiff word of welcome from the front seat.

"Ready?" his father asked no one in particular as he slid behind the wheel.

Byron closed his eyes and leaned his head against the cold side window. Next to him, Garrett was rocking in his seat and reciting the periodic table at the top of his lungs. Aside from his troubles adapting to his environment, Garrett didn't hear very well, and compensated by speaking loudly, the volume carrying in the confinement of the car.

His voice pierced through Byron's mind and intensified his pounding headache. He was in for a hellish drive to the airport. At least at this time in the morning, the traffic would be light.

Something slapped him against his forehead hard enough to sting. The back of Garrett's hand connected again with Byron's face.

I'm so tired of this shit.

Righting himself from his slumped position, he called his brother's name, "Garrett." Byron snapped his fingers in front of his brother. "Garrett!" He firmed his voice and winced as a spear stabbed at his temple. He snapped his fingers again, right in front of Garrett's face.

Faster than a snake, his brother bobbed forward and bit Byron's hand.

"Fucking hell," Byron yelled, setting off Garrett again, who screamed with a high-pitched voice.

Their mother half turned in the car and chastised Byron, "Mind your language and leave your brother alone."

Byron closed his eyes and breathed through his nose. It didn't work. Their mother always took sides, and Byron's temper flared. "Leave him alone? The stupid moron bit me." His voice rose in pitch.

"Byron," his father bit out, "language." At the same time, Garrett screeched like a banshee.

"Thomas!" The alarm in his mother's voice made Byron stiffen, and then his world skidded sideways and toppled over. Fragments of his father cursing, glass breaking, Garrett's high-pitched screaming, and the bone-crushing yank of the seatbelt filtered in before a heavy impact to the driver's side of the car sent them spinning the other way. Shock and pain as something slammed against his knee reverberated through Byron's lower body, and the car jostled and ground to a halt.

Disoriented, Byron shook his head. All he could hear was the ringing in his ears. *Have I gone deaf?* No, he could hear faint sounds: the hiss of liquid, car horns, skidding tires, brakes, frantic yelling outside the car. Outside! But inside, Garrett didn't scream, no reassuring words from their father, no breathing, crying, or moaning from his mother. Nothing to indicate there were other people besides him in the car. Warm liquid trickled down his face, and he tried to turn his head. Byron opened his mouth to speak, but with a feeling of tumbling back, his world turned black.

"Got one breathing here."

Someone lifted an eyelid—a flash of light, stabbing pain, then the oblivion of nothingness pulled him under again.

Jostling, yelling, a chain saw. *A what?*

Byron slid in and out of consciousness as the first responders worked to free him from the wreck. By now, the excruciating pain in his leg had turned into a throbbing numbness, and he was desperate to know how his family was doing, but he couldn't speak. He tried to swallow. A comforting hand landed on his shoulder and squeezed. "Don't try to move, buddy, we'll get you out."

Dad? Mom? G-Garrett?

He tried to call for them but only a weak moan, almost a whimper, left his mouth.

"Shh," someone soothed, "we know it hurts, but we need to know the damage before we move you." And then they did move him. Byron screamed in agony and blacked out again.

* * *

When he regained consciousness the next time, he was lying on his back with his head full of cotton. It felt like he was floating. Alarmed by his quiet surroundings and the smell of antiseptics, he tried to persuade his uncooperative mind into working.

Carefully, he opened an eye. He would have opened both, but one didn't seem to work. Byron knew he should worry about that inability, but his mind seemed as happy as a dreadlocked stoner singing reggae. He knew feeling happy and free was exceedingly wrong. Slowly, the sight from his one eye became less blurry, and his muddled brain tried to make sense of his surroundings.

Suddenly, a door opened and blinding light streamed in followed by a cheerful voice, "Oh good, you're awake."

Through parched lips, Byron tried to speak as a tall and lanky man in scrubs appeared in his line of sight.

The man fiddled with some controls and the head of the bed raised until Byron was almost in a sitting position. "Don't try to talk yet." Holding Byron's wrist in his hand, the man pressed two fingers on Byron's pulse point and looked at his watch. "You've been in an accident, but you're safe now. You shouldn't feel any pain but let me know if that changes." After a few seconds, the man let go of his wrist, and pulled a little penlight from the scrubs breast pocket. "Sorry about this."

Byron knew what was coming but still winced at the stabbing light. Luckily, this exam only took a few moments as well.

Byron tried to speak again, but all he could do was croak like a frog.

"Hold on." The man disappeared from Byron's vision and quickly reappeared, pushing a tray table with a cup and a clipboard on top. "Try a few of these." With practiced ease, he slipped some ice chips past Byron's lips.

They melted sweet on his tongue, and Byron couldn't remember ever being so thirsty. However, more than to quench his thirst, he was thirsty for information. "My-my dad?" he whispered hoarsely.

The man didn't speak but something in his expression made Byron try to struggle upright. "My mother?" Again, the man flinched. "Garrett?"

Same damn reaction. Byron's throat burned with unshed tears. The man squeezed his shoulder, looked up as the door opened again, and sighed. "I know you're doing your jobs, Officers, but I told you—"

"Yes, you did, and we cleared it with the doctor," an unfamiliar female spoke. Turning his head like he was an eighty-year-old cripple and not an eighteen-year-old athlete, Byron spotted two uniformed police officers.

A sturdy male officer made his way to the bed followed by his female partner. "I'm Officer Savino and this is Officer Rose. We were amongst the first responders on Route 435." He dipped his head to make eye contact with Byron. "You're probably aware that you're at the hospital and the doctor and nurses will take good care of you."

Byron's eyes slid to the female officer—what was her name again—and she nodded.

"We take it you're either Garrett or Byron Nolan?" Officer Savino's question pulled his attention back to the sturdy male.

"B-y-ron," he croaked.

Really? I look like a fucking thirteen-year-old?

Before he could voice his concerns about his family members, the woman—Officer Rose, he now remembered—spoke with an empathetic tone of voice, "We're very sorry to inform you that the others with you in the car sustained injuries they weren't able to survive."

Byron blinked as he processed her words. Dazed, he listened to the officers, robotically answering their questions until the man in scrubs ushered the policeman and policewoman out of the room with a firm, "You did your job, now let me do mine."

They left without a protest, although Officer Savino did manage to slip a card into Byron's uninjured hand and urged him to call if he needed anything.

"What a damn mess," Officer Rose muttered as they left the room. "The boy is too damn young to be on his own."

Her male partner hummed. "Such a stroke of bad luck. With the ice on the road, they didn't stand a chance."

But Byron knew better, he knew the cause of the accident and it sure wasn't bad luck. He clenched his fists around the blanket and squeezed his eyes shut. A warm tear trickled down his uninjured cheek.

He wasn't sure how much time had passed since his mind had slipped into the past. He talked about the event, he talked about his brother, his parents, and finally about his shame and guilt. He spoke until his voice was a bit hoarse, swallowing hard when the last of a story he'd never expected to share was finally uttered.

Charlotte didn't move or talk, just listened as the beautiful, strong man revealed the scars the accident left, the scars that weren't visible on the outside but cut the deepest.

"What you told me about Garrett…" She chewed her lip and tried to figure out how to phrase it delicately, before plunging forward. "He wasn't just hearing impaired, was he?"

Although she couldn't see him move, snuggled against his chest as she was, she sensed him shake his head.

"No, Garrett had several issues. He was diagnosed with Classic Autistic Disorder and had epilepsy." Byron's chest heaved with a mighty sigh. "He needed constant help and attention and had a profound need for routine. He used to rock in his chair and recite the chemical elements from the periodic table. It always drove me nuts." His voice trailed off.

Idly stroking his bicep, Charlotte waited for him to continue.

"Garrett got upset by change in his routine and I was running late. So, he was super agitated by the time we started to drive. I should have left him alone and ignored him. I didn't and they paid."

Charlotte leaned back in his hold and tipped her head to look up at him. "Do you truly think you're responsible? You weren't driving. You didn't control the weather."

"But the fight between Garrett and me distracted my father."

"Possibly, but people get distracted often. Have you never missed something in traffic because your mind wandered or because you were changing radio stations or answering your phone?"

"Sure," he said with a slight shrug.

Not convinced she was really reaching him, she said, "Was that the only time you and your brother ever fought in the car?"

He snorted. "Of course not. We were kids..."

She watched as his expression began to change.

"What I'm saying is that while your fight might have distracted your dad, that most likely happened many times before without any consequences. The difference this time was the condition of the road. Even without your fight, the car could have easily slid out of control on the ice." She placed her hand on his marred cheek. "Let it go, darling."

His mouth trembled slightly, and she swung her arms around his neck. They sat for a long time. Long enough for the sweat on her back to cool, but she didn't mind the chill one bit if she could help him get rid of the guilt and shame. She was aware it wouldn't happen this night, but hoped that, over time, he would come to terms with what happened with a guilt-free conscience and a more adult perspective of the event.

DAY TWENTY-EIGHT

After an initial meeting with the divorce lawyer, Byron led Charlotte into Nolan House with his hand splayed on the small of her back. He'd just greeted Dan at the door, when commotion behind them made his steps falter and his head turned to peek over his shoulder. Tall enough to spot what—or rather who—was causing the ruckus, Byron sped up, wanting to get Charlotte inside the building as quickly as possible.

"What's the matter?" Instead of picking up the pace, she slowed down and started to turn around.

"Keep walking. Liam"—he spat the name the name with all the loathing and disgust he felt for the bastard—"is behind us, no doubt intent on causing a scene."

At his information, she paled and hurried forward. Unfortunately, her rush to get inside messed with her coordination, and Charlotte stumbled over the threshold, almost falling. Byron made a grab for her, which prevented a "face meets marble floor" disaster, but from her pained yelp and her stumbled step, he couldn't keep her from twisting her ankle.

Byron scooped her into his arms, despite her frantic, "your leg," and had almost cleared the door when their elderly doorman, Dan, was pushed and stumbled into Byron's side.

Screaming and cursing like a madman, Liam slammed a fist into Byron's right kidney, and immediately, muscle spasms shot up Byron's spine, a wave of nausea hitting him. With Charlotte in his arms, he was virtually defenseless because he wasn't going to let go of her or turn away from the madman. He threw himself forward through the door and relief washed over him when he spotted Earl racing toward them, one hand on his earpiece —no doubt calling for back-up.

"You give her back to me, you bastard!" Liam yelled. Flailing his arms, he shoved Dan again, before punching the kind older man in the face.

"No!" Charlotte struggled in his arms.

Did she want to take the bastard on and defend the doorman? Oh yes, she would. Not knowing if he should be irritated or proud, Byron tightened his grip on her and shushed, "Shh, baby, Earl and the others will take care of this."

He winced as Earl sidestepped a wild swing and planted a well-aimed punch in Liam's soft belly. The asshole folded in half on an "Oomph," and two other security workers rushed outside to secure the lunatic.

"Sir," Earl's voice carried into the building, "do you want to press charges?"

"Absolutely, can you look after Dan as well?" He pressed Charlotte's face against the crook of his neck. "I need to take care of my woman."

"Of course, Sir."

Limping more pronouncedly than normal, he carried Charlotte through the private hallway to the elevator and punched in the code. He peered down at the trembling woman he held close and flexed his arms when she voiced her concern for him and demanded to be let down. He frowned and shook his head admonishingly. "I'm not letting you put weight on that foot, and did you just give me an order?"

"Just shoot me now." Still trembling from the encounter and the explosion of violence, she tried to glare at him. "He punched you in the back, and you worry about a twisted ankle? It barely hurts. And what about your doorman? He's just a sweet old guy, who has done nothing to no one."

"Earl and his team will take care of Dan, the cops, and your asshole-ex. I'm taking care of you!"

The elevator doors slid open, and Byron stepped inside without letting go of her—beloved, stubborn, domineering man. Fearing that if she struggled, she would hurt him even more, Charlotte swallowed her protest and kept herself very still.

The elevator whooshed to the penthouse silently, and neither of them spoke as Byron carried her straight through to the bathroom before lowering her to the floor, making sure she kept the weight off her injured leg.

He bent to close the lid to the toilet seat, winced, and contorted his back as he shuddered with pain. "Sit," he ordered.

She braced herself on the vanity. "You should sit down yourself."

"Kitten."

She sighed, performed a half pirouette on her uninjured foot, and planted her butt on the closed toilet. "Will you at least let me check your back when you've had your way?"

He knelt and shrugged. "Sure." With careful but sure hands, he removed her shoe and checked the damage.

"Don't worry, I had worse from Liam."

A low growl escaped his throat.

Uh oh, wrong thing to say.

Despite her protests, Byron insisted on wrapping her ankle and getting an icepack from the kitchen.

Finally satisfied and sure she was sufficiently taken care of, Byron relented and allowed her to take care of him.

Charlotte slipped her hands over his chest and to the buttons of his shirt. Maintaining eye contact, she unfastened the first button. Trailing her finger up the exposed skin, she worked her way down until she'd unbuttoned each one. Byron tried to look impassive, but she didn't miss his wince when he shrugged out of the shirt.

"I can see you're hurting, darling." She leaned forward and pressed a tender kiss over his heart. "Please turn around." Her eyes watered as he did, and she could see the fist-size bruising already forming on his lower back. "It's a wonder he didn't take out your kidney."

Byron nodded. "Yeah, he got me good."

"Tell me what I can do to make it better."

He half turned and gave her a lopsided smile. "I can survive a bruised kidney, Kittycat, because you're with me."

She inwardly melted.

"Having you with me settles me," Byron continued. "Having you with me means you're not with that abusive asshole. You're safe and I can take care of you."

She pulled in a breath. *He loves me and wants to*

keep me safe. His discomfort means nothing to him when it means preventing me from getting hurt.

Slowly he bobbed his head. "And now you understand, kitten? Finally, realize how much you mean to me?"

It was her turn to nod. "I do," she said, her voice turning husky. "And I love you, too." Her gaze dropped to the bruise.

Without a word, he handed her a tube of arnica salve and a small brown bottle from the first aid kit.

"I recognize the salve, but what's in the bottle?"

"It's Frankincense essential oil; add a drop to the salve."

"Seriously?"

"Believe me, it's the best."

She squeezed a dollop of salve on her index finger and added a drop of the oil before carefully dabbing it on the bruise. Although the injury upset her and she was bone tired, she didn't miss the broad expanse of his back and the rippling of muscles. He really was a beautiful man, inside and out.

"Done!" After she recapped the bottle and tube and washed her hands, Byron lifted her in his arms and carried her to the bed where he arranged them with her leg propped up over his hip.

29

DAY TWENTY-NINE

"Hold on a second," Byron said.

Charlotte had turned to question him on the order when she realized he was speaking on his phone as he returned to the office. He tossed the phone on top of his desk, and she squealed when she found herself being separated from the floor as her Master simply scooped her off her feet. The folder she'd been about to slide into its place in the file cabinet was plucked from her hand and tossed onto a nearby chair.

"What are you doing?" she asked as she slipped her arms around his neck.

"You're still favoring your ankle." He carried her around his desk. Settling her on his lap, he took her foot in his hand, easing off her shoe and gently wrapping his fingers around her ankle.

Her heart hitched at the thought of all she was

going to miss when she left tomorrow. She couldn't care less about the penthouse, drivers, five-star restaurants, designer clothing, or the balance of his bank account. This was all that mattered. A man who honestly cared about her, who saw things she didn't even notice herself. A man whose simple touch could make her body heat whether he was massaging her ankle or stroking his fingers over her nakedness.

"How does it feel?"

His question jolted her back to the moment. "Fabulous," she replied drowsily, and at his chuckle, realized he was asking about her ankle and not the massage. "It's fine, really." She rotated her foot as if to add to the veracity of her statement. "How's your back?"

"It's okay."

She narrowed her eyes at his non-committal answer, doubting it was entirely true. She'd seen the discoloration of the bruising when he'd dressed that morning. Instead of calling him out though, she gestured to the phone that he seemed to have forgotten. "Who's on the phone?"

"Your lawyer."

She smacked his shoulder. "And you put her on hold? Are you crazy! Don't lawyers charge like a zillion dollars a minute?"

Byron chuckled. "More like a hundred, but I wanted you to hear this. Ready?"

Not really. But what she said was, "I guess I'm going to have to become used to speaking with her, so I suppose I'm as ready as I'll ever be."

"Relax, everything is going to be fine." He bent to brush his lips over hers. He proved he honestly didn't care about the pending legal bill as he didn't pull away for several minutes. When he finally released her, it was her turn to have forgotten the phone until he punched some buttons and Charlotte saw another desk come into view. This one had an attractive middle-aged woman sitting behind it.

"Okay, Daniella, Charlotte has joined us, so you can fill us both in." Byron tightened his arm around her when she attempted to rise off his lap.

"Good evening, Charlotte."

"Um… good evening," Charlotte stuttered, a bit startled the call included video but when her lawyer didn't appear the least bit fazed at seeing her sitting on Byron's lap, Charlotte relaxed and settled more comfortably against Master's broad chest.

"After yesterday's altercation at the Nolan Building, this morning Byron suggested I have our investigator delve more deeply into your husband's activities. It didn't take him long to uncover some rather some serious allegations."

"You mean Liam's attempted to attack someone else?" Charlotte's eyebrows rose.

"Not exactly, though I'm not ruling anything

out. I can't go into all the details yet, but I can disclose that Byron isn't the only one of Randall's business associates who have expressed concern about dealings with Randall. Several others are threatening him with charges ranging from alleged embezzlement to outright fraud."

"What does that mean?" Charlotte asked, looking not at the phone but up at her Master.

"It means Liam's ass is grass, right, Dannie?" Byron rumbled without a trace of pity as he bent to brush a kiss to Charlotte's forehead.

The sound of Daniella's light laugh drew their attention. "Well, that's not exactly a legal term, but if the shoe fits." She shrugged. "We still have a lot of work to do, but while it's not looking good for your husband—"

"*Ex*-husband," Byron cut in with a growl that had Charlotte smiling and Daniella laughing again.

"Soon to be ex-husband," Daniella amended, her own smile growing as she focused her attention on her client. "It is very good news for you, Charlotte. I just wanted to keep you up to date and will let you know more as the investigation develops."

"Thank you, Ms. Wilson," Charlotte said softly, feeling lighter than she had since deciding to end her marriage.

"Yes, thank you, Dannie. We'll talk later." At Daniella's goodbye, Byron ended the call and wrapped his arms around Charlotte, stroking his finger down her arm when she sighed deeply. "What's wrong?"

"How could I not know that Liam is a criminal? Am I really that dense?"

"No, Kittycat, you were attempting to survive," Byron's reply came without a moment's hesitation. "Don't consider for a second that you should have known. The man fooled a lot of people." Byron rubbed his hands over her arms in a comforting gesture. "Now, enough about the ass. My concern is you. Are you all right?"

"I will be." She reached up to cup his cheek with her hand. "Thank you, Master."

"I didn't do anything." He took her hand and kissed her palm.

"You've done far more than you'll ever know." She slid her hand from his but only in order to slip it behind his head to guide his mouth to hers. He might not believe her words, but she hoped he understood the depth of her gratitude in her kiss.

The growl she heard didn't come from Master, but was loud enough for him to pull back, a grin on his face as she felt hers heat with color. "I guess it's time for me to start dinner," she said, pressing her hand to her complaining empty stomach.

"No need. I'd already placed an order to be delivered before Daniella called—I hope you like Thai food."

She nodded.

"Tonight, we're going to take it easy and enjoy ourselves." He bent forward and captured her lips. If strength and masculine confidence had a flavor, she was tasting it now.

Tonight will be our last night. What will my future be like? Will I be able to divorce Liam? She put her thoughts in a mental box and closed the virtual lid decisively. She refused to ruin her last night with pointless worries.

When he pulled back, she said, "Thai sounds lovely." She attempted to reach around his neck and pull him back to her, but he captured her hands in his. She pressed her bottom lip forward, and the pout made him laugh.

"There will be enough time for that later, Kitty-cat. First, I need to feed you." He pushed himself up. "You'll need the energy." He cradled her in his arms with one arm supporting her back and the other her legs.

"Byron," she squealed, "I can walk."

"I know." He nuzzled her neck and carried her out of the office and straight to the kitchen.

"Well, put me down then," she sassed—secretly hoping he would never let her go.

"Nope."

She tipped back her head to see his smile. He smiled so much more these days.

Instead of carrying her over to the dining table,

he placed her on the kitchen counter. She arched an eyebrow.

"I'm too eager to get you in bed to sit down for dinner."

"So why bother?"

His brow furrowed. "You need to eat. You barely ate all day." He pulled containers from a plastic take-out bag, and the delicious scent of lemongrass, chilies, garlic, ginger, coconut milk, coriander, and cumin wafted from the food.

As if on cue, her stomach growled again.

"See?" He chuckled as he left her on the counter and went to the drawer with cutlery. "Pad Thai?" He pointed the fork at her favorite dish.

She bobbed her head eagerly, and he scooped up a forkful of and held it in front of her mouth.

The rich flavor of delicious pad Thai sauce exploded on her tongue, as she chewed the rice noodles, shrimp, chicken, peanuts, a scrambled egg, and bean sprouts. She watched him take a bite for himself and bit back a moan as his lips engulfed the fork she just ate from.

He alternated between them until they emptied the container.

"Done?"

She nodded and licked her lips, catching a stray drop of sauce. "Thank you, that was delicious."

He kept his eyes riveted on the spot she just

licked. Charlotte placed her hands on the countertop behind her back and tried to look down.

A single finger under her chin tipped her head back, and his blue fire seared into her. "You know you don't have to leave, right?"

Heaving out a sigh, she shook her head. "You're wrong about that. I feel I have to. I need to do this on my own."

"How often have I told you that I love you?" he asked softly.

She wrinkled her nose and avoided eye contact. "You told me a lot. And I love you, too," she hurried to say, "but that doesn't mean I can stay, Byron. I need to divorce Liam, and I need to stand on my own two feet. I've become so dependent on him. I —" She chewed her bottom lip. "Just, can we not talk about this tonight? I want to forget everything for one night."

His scar creased as one side of his mouth tipped up at the corner. "That we can do." He kissed the tip of her nose.

* * *

After feeding his kitten, Byron carried her back to his room. If tonight was going to be their last night, he should make it something worthwhile, and he had some interesting toys he hadn't introduced her to yet.

The sexual energy practically hummed between them, and he was grateful for the loose fit of his cotton drawstring pants—in jeans, he would be in agony right now.

As he placed her in the middle of his bed, she gave him a warm smile. She was comfortable enough with him to give herself to him and relinquish control. They'd come so far in building trust in only a month.

A trust he reveled in and gladly accepted. But she wasn't the only one who'd learned to trust—who'd let go of a horrendous past. He had never been so close to a person that he wanted to talk about his scars. That explanation had to wait, though. Tonight, he wanted to indulge in her body one last time before they would say their farewell. A farewell he was determined to make an "until we meet again," although he respected and even understood her need to make it on her own.

Since he didn't do anything halfway, Byron would keep an eye on her. And he would protect her from her soon-to-be ex.

Pushing the bastard firmly from his mind, he surveyed his submissive. "I want you in the Humble position, facing the headboard. For tonight, I plan bondage, light spanking, and toys—all pleasurable, Kittycat."

"All right, Sir."

Her eager acceptance and the prompt and

graceful way she slid into the requested position, increased his regret their agreement was ending. The penthouse would become a lot colder after tomorrow.

Suppressing a sigh, he took rope and toys from his closet, including one of his favorites.

He placed his good knee next to her on the mattress, stroked her back, and fondled her bottom. "Such a good kitten, offering her body up for her Master's use." With firm hands, he teased the Ben Wa balls through her folds gathering up wetness. Although she let out a moan, she kept perfectly in place, and he kissed her neck as he slid the two balls inside. "Don't lose them."

Her muscles tightened. "I'll do my best, Sir."

He grinned. "I know." He slapped her bottom lightly, spreading out the spanks, and warming her entire backside until her asscheeks held a nice rosy-pink glow. He checked her face. She had closed her eyes and parted her lips. Her cheeks glowed as pink as her bottom.

Indulging himself and her, he took her mouth in a long, searing kiss, while fondling her breasts.

He kept his knee to the mattress and resisted the urge to join her on the bed. His control was so close to snapping, he needed the barrier. First, he wanted to play with her. After tonight it would be a while before he could touch her how and when he wanted.

He pulled back from her and helped her into a sitting position. Using two lengths of rope, he tied her breasts in a simple but efficient breast harness, making sure his hands were on her the entire time. He stroked the sides of her breasts, circled the areolas until they puckered and bunched, and took his sweet time to stroke the sensitive undersides of her mounds.

He stroked his knuckles over her scorching hot cheek. "Ready for more?"

Her eyelids lifted and her pupils were dilated so wide, they almost swallowed the emerald green.

He slid his hands over her body, all the way to her pussy. The Ben Wa balls were already doing a fine job in lubricating her. Her muscles went rigid, and her breathing became labored. He nudged her legs farther apart, opening her pussy wider for him. "I don't want to tie you." He wanted to see her squirm and struggle to obey. "But I want you to keep your hands against the mattress and your legs spread wide, can you do that?"

"I'm not sure, but I will try."

"Yes, you will. When you don't obey me, I will punish you with orgasm denial, and I'd much rather give you multiple orgasms tonight."

Her hands fisted in the bedsheets, and opening her legs even wider, she hooked her ankles around the edge of the bed. Clever Kittycat.

He rose from the bed and plugged the powerful wand vibrator into a socket.

He stroked the bulbous head through her swollen folds. She was very wet, and when he pulled back the device, the top was glistering with her juices. He clicked through the settings and settled on a deep, slow purring. As soon as he touched the tip of the wand to her clit, she clamped her legs together in a reflex.

"Bad Kittycat. That's one punishment."

She shot him a disgruntled glare and he smirked. "Glaring at your Master will only rack up the punishment."

Oh, she tried to contain her angry gaze, she truly did, but it only made her expression more exasperating.

He stroked a hand over her slit and pushed a finger into her.

She cried out and arched her back at the intrusion.

"Don't move." He placed the vibrator back against her clit and leisurely teased his finger in and out her hot, snug pussy.

He clicked the switch several times and surveyed her body language and facial expressions like a predator watches its prey. When she tightened her legs muscles at one setting, he stopped and pressed the vibrating head against her pink swollen bud.

Immediately, her cunt clamped down on his finger and the Ben Wa balls vibrated inside.

He waited for her to near the pinnacle, held, and removed the vibrator and his finger just before she could go over the edge.

Caressing the sensitive skin above her hipbones, he gave her time to come down from her near climax, and she wiggled as his strokes turned into a tickling sensation.

Her high breasts wobbled nicely with each breath, and he slid his hands up her body and cupped the small mounds. Women's breasts were so fascinating—round, firm, and yet soft. He bent forward to nuzzle between them, and to lick and suckle on the salty skin.

"Sir, please," she pleaded, "please, Master, pleaszz…" The last word ended on a whine.

"All right, little kitten. I think you're more than ready to come, right?"

"Yess. Yes, Sir. Please."

He flicked the switch on the magic wand. "Oh, believe me. This will be entirely my pleasure." He pressed the wand hard against her completely exposed and engorged clit until she fell right into a mind-blowing orgasm.

He didn't pull back the wand but rode her climax with her until the twitching of her hips became evasive rather than in pleasure.

All tension left her body, and he placed the wand

back against her pussy. "Time for another one, kitten, before I will take you for my own pleasure." Byron didn't know when the next time after tonight would be, and he was going to take her as if she were his last meal. They might have just one night left, but their time together wasn't over yet.

30

DAY THIRTY

Charlotte forced back her tears as she saw the dress slacks and blouse Byron laid out for her to wear. Oh, the material and fit were beautiful, and the colors would suit her to a T, but they were vanilla street clothes and emphasized she was leaving today.

She swallowed hard and fought tears as she dressed.

I don't want to go.

She went over to the kitchen and froze as she spotted Byron at the stove.

"Sir?"

"Ah"—he turned with a spatula in his hand —"there you are. The blouse is lovely on you. Why don't you have a seat, so we can eat?"

Seat? She'd gotten used to being on his lap or

kneeling beside his chair as they ate the breakfast she prepared. Like a soldier crossing a minefield, she went over to the chair and lowered herself onto the seat.

Folding her hands in her lap, she lowered her head as if in prayer. Movement in her peripheral vision startled her and she glanced up. Byron had placed a plate with her favorite foods in front of her on the table. She wasn't the least bit hungry, however.

The coffeemaker whirled and roared, hot air spluttered, and the smell of warm milk and dark espresso filled the kitchen.

A mug appeared beside her plate, and Byron slid onto the chair on the opposite side of the table.

As if he wants to put as much distance between us as possible.

"Please." His tone was cordial, and she looked up to see him indicating her plate. "Eat."

Charlotte lifted her fork and shoved the food around the plate. She dropped the utensil without taking a bite and took a sip of the cappuccino instead.

"If you're not going to eat, then talk to me." Byron lifted his own cup to his mouth and studied her over the rim. "Have you decided what you're going to do?"

She shrugged.

"You're welcome to stay, Kittycat."

"You know I can't." Swallowing her tears, she shook her head. "I'm not returning to my husband, but I need to stand on my own two feet."

"At least come work for me."

"No." The word came out harsher than she intended and hurt flashed over his face.

How could I have pegged this man for cold and heartless?

She held up a placating hand. "Sorry, that wasn't what I meant to say. I would love to come and work for you, but if we end up together, you and me both will always wonder if my decision was from free will, laziness, or desperation."

"You're not lazy."

"No, I'm not." Amusement tickled the corners of her mouth.

Amazing how he can make me smile —even now.

Bravely, she reached over the table, slid her palm against his hand, and interlaced their fingers. "In my head, I've always believed Liam and Michael as they trash-talked me. I allowed them to have power over me. I will never allow anyone to make me doubt myself again." She squeezed his hand as he opened his mouth, and he stayed silent. "I love when you take control, and I'm definitely a submissive. However, I want to discover more about myself before I jump into another relationship. Meanwhile, I can go to secretary school and get some counseling."

Now it was Byron's turn to squeeze her fingers. "I'm proud of you, Kittycat, and even with how much it pains me to let you leave, I understand why you have to do so."

"You do?"

For the first time that morning, he smiled and tilted his head.

Oh yes, he did! She swallowed around the lump in her throat. "I love you."

His entire face brightened with joy before his expression softened with affection. "I love you too, Kittycat—enough to let you go"—he paused and added—"for now." He released her hand, picked up his fork, and pointed it at her plate. "Now eat before the food gets cold and tell me about your plans."

And so, Charlotte talked. Humming and nodding, Byron mostly listened and occasionally offered advice and assistance. There wasn't a shred of doubt in her mind that he would be there for her, whatever her decisions would be, and maybe this would work out. "So, secretary school is nine months, but the classes don't start until February. It will give me enough time to find a place to live and a part-time job to pay the rent."

A thoughtful expression took over his face. "That will mean you'll have your diploma in about one year from now."

She nodded. "Yes. It isn't going to be easy, but my life with Liam wasn't easy either. However, I'm not going to dwell on my mistakes. I can't turn back time. There isn't a way to travel back, not even to a location because time inevitably will have changed the place from what I remember. Instead, I will go ahead and look forward."

He took her hand in his again. "I'm so proud of you, and I'm certain you're going to make a success of everything you decide to do with your life. I will give you the time and space you apparently need because I want what's best for you. What I think is best for you might not be the same as what you think, but I'm not you and I have my own experiences and past to cloud my judgment. Also... my special future-showing binoculars are broken. What I want to say, my advice—although well-meaning—is colored and will hardly help you on the path you have to go. I love you, Kittycat, whatever you choose to do. Trust your heart, what does it tell you to do?"

He meant every word and she was so over-whelmed and happy she couldn't speak. Awkwardly, while still holding hands with him, she got up, rounded the table, and straddled his lap. They kissed and cuddled for a long time, their breakfast forgotten.

When they finally came up for air, he gave her a heart-meltingly sweet peck on her nose and whis-pered, "One year, Kittycat." He leaned his forehead against hers. "I'll give you one year to work on your goals and then I'm coming for you."

They sat in silence, both lost in their own thoughts. Although she was a bit sad, hope also soared in her heart.

EPILOGUE

31

ONE YEAR LATER

"Don't make it too late, boss lady." Estella, her efficient administrative assistant leaned her shoulder
against the doorpost of Charlotte's office.

Charlotte checked the time at the top of her
computer screen. "Heck, you're right." She saved the
file and logged out of the system.

"You seemed to be pleased with yourself," Estella
observed as she handed Charlotte her lightweight
coat.

"I am pleased. Randall Estate is making a little
profit this month despite all the renovations and
upgrades we needed to do."

Liam's sins had finally caught up to him when
one of his many business partners caught him
embezzling funds. That had led to further audits
and investigations racking up a long list of convic-

tions and eventual incarceration. He'd not survived more than three nights in prison when he upset the wrong gang on his arrival. Since he never made a testament and her lawyer hadn't yet filed for a divorce, Charlotte inherited his entire business and discovered he made money with as little regard for others as he treated her and their marriage. She'd been working to make things right since the solicitor disclosed she'd become the owner.

"Already? You only took over the reins five months ago." Estella held open the office door and arched an eyebrow. "And despite you getting rid of the most profitable assets?"

"Assets," Charlotte scoffed, her heels clicking on the tiled hallway floor as she and her assistant made their way to the exit. "Count on Liam and Michael to be ripping off people who aren't capable of defending themselves."

Estella gave her a sideways glance and smiled. "But you're setting it right."

"Yes"—Charlotte's spine straightened—"I am."

"I'm proud of you, boss lady."

Charlotte's step faltered for a moment, but she picked up the brisk pace and nodded. "You know, I'm proud of myself, too, though I never actually finished school."

They halted in front of the bank of elevators and Estella pressed the button to go down. "When would you have had the time to finish? Besides, you nailed the GED test with flying colors, right? You're too hard on yourself."

Charlotte just hummed and watched the lighted numbers above the left elevator change. The doors slid open, and they stepped inside and turned in unison to face the exit.

For a few moments, they stood in comfortable silence beside each other as the elevator started its fast descent before Charlotte turned to her trusted assistant. "So, it's Friday night. Do you have any exciting plans?"

Estella launched into a description of her plans involving bars and dancing and—as usual—suggested, "Why don't you come with me? You could do with some winding down and perhaps even celebrate."

Charlotte's answer was postponed as they stepped off the elevator and started toward the exit. Both waved at the night security guard as they walked past the desk and the entry door slid open.

"I don't know," Charlotte hedged. Stepping outside the building, she squinted against the afternoon sun and scanned her surroundings. The self-defense training, Byron insisted she followed, taught her well.

Estella argued—also their usual—that Charlotte needed downtime during the weekend, and Charlotte listened with a half ear because she was expecting her weekend was about to get claimed.

As soon as she spotted the sleek Tesla at the curb, her heart began to hammer. Charlotte placed a hand on Estella's arm and interrupted her mid-sentence. "Sorry, Ella, I'm going to beg a rain check on that drink."

Estella followed Charlotte's line of sight and grinned. "Oh, the mystery man of the daily flowers and weekly gifts has finally arrived?"

"Yes, that's Byron's car." Charlotte bit her lip and restlessly shifted her feet on the pavement.

"Well, boss lady"—Estella bumped her shoulder with Charlotte's—"what are you waiting for? Go get your man."

Her man!

The winglike back doors of the Model X slid up, and Charlotte hoped she'd remembered to wish Estella a good evening because the next moment she was moving.

A shiny shoe appeared, followed by a long leg in navy blue suit pants.

Her feet moved faster.

A strong hand with long fingers curled around the doorframe.

Despite her heels, she turned her walk into a jog. Dignity be damned!

The late afternoon sun reflected off a cuff link as

Byron fully rose from the backseat and turned toward Charlotte just in time to open his arms to catch her.

She flung herself at him with a whoop, and he caught her against his chest with a chuckle. "Missed me, eh?"

Charlotte grabbed his beloved, scarred face between both hands and whispered against his lips, "Like crazy." Brazenly, she leaned forward and pressed their lips together.

Byron's arms flexed and his hold tightened, and she enjoyed his strength and how she affected him.

Teasing her tongue over his bottom lip, she requested entrance, and he opened for her on a sigh. For the first time in a year, she tasted his innate masculinity with a hint of black coffee and breathed in his amber scent. It was like her body had been in a coma and the sensory input sprang her back to life, and Charlotte became acutely aware of her female body parts. When they broke free, both were panting.

She smiled against his lips. "Did you miss me?"

"Kittycat, I missed you every second of each minute, every minute of each hour, every hour in each day, every day of each week, every week of each month, and every month of the entire fucking year." He rested his forehead again hers. "Please, don't leave me again."

"I won't, Sir."

He let her slide down his body, and she reveled in every ridge and dip of his hard, toned body.

I'm looking forward to getting reacquainted with every inch of him later.

Meanwhile, Byron had taken her hand and sank down on his good knee.

What? Her eyes widened.

"Don't make me wait any longer for you." He swallowed and held out a small velvet box. "Marry me."

Speechless, Charlotte stared at his beloved face. A tear trailed down her cheek. Byron's face relaxed and his eyes softened. She slowly nodded. More tears followed the first. She bobbed her head faster and held out her hand.

Byron's hands shook when he removed the ring and slid it on the third finger of her left hand. He bent and pressed a kiss to her knuckles. "Please accept this ring as a symbol of my promise, my devotion, and my everlasting love."

Charlotte stared at the ring on her finger and mused, "I can hardly believe what all happened last year not to mention how our relationship started. You made a wicked deal, Sir."

Byron rose to his feet and engulfed her in his arms. "To the best deal I made in my life."

The End

If you enjoyed this story, please consider leaving a review and follow Karen Nappa on Goodreads for more hot stories!

ABOUT THE AUTHOR

Karen Nappa is an Amazon bestselling author of Seasoned BDSM romance with HEA. Her books are available at the popular retailers and include series such as the Club Indigo series and The Quinn Quartet.

Immersed in the D/s lifestyle herself, she writes realistic albeit romantic stories. When not dominated by her cats or her Master (in that order—even if it earns her a spanking!), she loves going places to discover the stories waiting to be written.

She resides in the Netherlands with her dominant husband, two adult-ish sons—and whoever they might drag home with them—and, of course, her two Chausie cats. If she isn't writing or texting with friends, she's probably reading, running, or listening to heavy metal.

Follow her on BookBub or download a free book and sign-up for her newsletter and never miss another release.

Website: https://www.karennappa.com

Twitter: https://www.twitter.com/karennappa

Instagram: https://www.instagram.com/karennappaauthor/

Facebook: https://m.facebook.com/authorkarennappa/

BookBub: https://www.bookbub.com/authors/karen-nappa?follow=true

Newsletter: https://author-karen-nappa.mailerpage.com/freebies

ALSO BY KAREN NAPPA

Do you enjoy Seasoned BDSM Romance with HEA?

Check out Club Indigo as well!

Trapped (Club Indigo #1)

Trusted (Club Indigo #2)

Appreciated (Club Indigo #3)

Cherished (Club Indigo #4)

Sonja's Confession (Club Indigo #4.5)

Blinded (Club Indigo #5)

United (Club Indigo #6)

A Mistress for Christmas (Club Indigo #6.5)

Conflicted (Club Indigo #7)

Diamonds and Rubies (Club Indigo #7.5)

How about interconnected small town romantic suspense?

Things might look Peaceful on the surface, but danger lies beneath.

Healing Jacob's Heart: a prequel to the Quinn Quartet

Delving Deep (The Quinn Quartet #1)

Finding Trouble (The Quinn Quartet #2)

Standing Fast (The Quinn Quartet #3)

Facing Consequences (The Quinn Quartet #4)

Karen Nappa is also part of...

Lust has no age limit!

A Season for Love Anthology

RED HOT ROMANCE

We at Red Hot Romance Publishing would like to thank you for your interest in our books.

If you liked this book (or even if you didn't), we appreciate your taking the time to leave a review on whichever site you purchased it. Reviews provide useful feedback in the form of positive comments and constructive criticism, which allows us to make sure we're providing the content our customers enjoy reading.

To check out more books from Red Hot Romance Publishing, to learn more about our publishing house, or to join our mailing list, please visit our website at:

http://www.redhotromancepublishing.com

Printed in Great Britain
by Amazon

41899089R00169